WOLFGANG KOEPPEN

YOUTH:
AUTOBIOGRAPHICAL WRITINGS

TRANSLATED BY
MICHAEL HOFMANN

T0161767

⊡ **DALKEY ARCHIVE PRESS**
Champaign / London / Dublin

Youth, originally published in German as 'Jugend' by Suhrkamp, Frankfurt am Main, 1976;
Once Upon a Time in Masuria originally published in German as 'Es war einmal in Masuren',
Suhrkamp, 1991

Library of Congress Cataloging-in-Publication Data
Koeppen, Wolfgang, 1906-1996, author.
[Jungend. English]
Youth : autobiographical writings / Wolfgang Koeppen. -- First edition.
    pages cm
ISBN 978-1-62897-050-0 (pbk. : acid-free paper)
1. Koeppen, Wolfgang, 1906---Childhood and youth. 2. Authors, German--20th
century--Biography. I. Hofmann, Michael, 1957 August 25- translator. II. Title.
PT2621.O46Z46 2014
833'.912--dc23
[B]
                    2014016366

Partially funded by the Illinois Arts Council, a state agency
and the University of Illinois at Urbana-Champaign

www.dalkeyarchive.com

Printed on permanent/durable acid-free paper
Cover: design and composition Mikhail Iliatov

YOUTH:
AUTOBIOGRAPHICAL WRITINGS

Table of Contents

Translator's Preface

In the winter of 1992, I visited Wolfgang Koeppen in his high, gloomy, cavernous apartment on the banks of Munich's green rushing river, the Isar, to give him a copy of my new translation of his novel, *Death in Rome*. Many things about that afternoon, which was dark when it began and soon turned into evening, might have been calculated to cause vertigo and bewilderment. I was there ostensibly to "interview" him, which was not something I'd ever done before. I had and have the deepest admiration for his writing—especially the so-called "post-War trilogy" of *Pigeons on the Grass* (1951), *The Hothouse* (1953), and the book I had begun by translating, *Death in Rome* (1954—Koeppen was someone who wrote his books quickly and in little clusters, or not at all). It was all so long ago in his life, and before the beginning of mine—but what else was there to talk about? *Death in Rome* was and remained his last novel. Then there was Koeppen's age, he was in his mid-80s, fifty years my senior: how to show respect and forbearance to such a man, and yet extract some information from him for the readers of the *Observer*? His long life was full of old mysteries. Uninquisitive and content with the books, I didn't know what they were: how he got through the War; the mystery of his writing and not-writing; his long, torturous marriage to a woman who, when he married her, was under-age—that was something else it certainly wouldn't have occurred to me to question him about. And yet here was someone who had haunted 1920s Berlin, the *Romanisches Café* and all—who spoke with real feeling for the lost decades of German-Jewish civilization, who, himself a young man in his twenties, claimed to have met Joseph Roth, whom I had also lately begun translating, and who had always seemed inconceivably remote to me, until I found myself sitting in the company of this man who had once been his younger colleague!

With my English reticence and youth, I met Koeppen half-way: in other words, we were both barely out of our shells. He was quietly plangent, courtly, a little dusty (literally, not in the sense of "dusty answer"), eerily patient. He gave me six hours of his time. I had a piece of paper on my knee, and tried to write down whatever struck me in what he said. Much of the time we must have been silent, some of it with me scribbling. What spoke to me was the décor, the stage-managed layout (Koeppen had a background in the theater)—though he didn't show me around, and I of course didn't ask to be shown. A sense of dim rooms going off in two or three directions, each one with a writing table in it, each writing table equipped with a bright table-lamp and a typewriter, each typewriter with a piece of paper in it, scrolled half-down and written upon, everywhere a key practically in mid-stroke, mid-letter, mid-air. How could one man keep all these rooms and tables and typewriters happy? It suggested a kind of literary Jackson Pollock, hitting the ground, when at all, running. The appearance of an unremitting productiveness, a ghost factory, a grand alibi. If I had read it at the time, it might have reminded me of the scene in Koeppen's first novel, *A Sad Affair* (1934) in which Friedrich, his autobiographical hero, is set to work nights in a light bulb factory, replacing bulbs as they burn out in experimental circuits. Presumably, Koeppen would not have done much more than that, going the rounds of his sites of production, replacing the bulbs, feeding, depending on your point of view, a delicious refusal or a wretched hoax.

Because there were no novels after 1954. In 1958, 1959, and 1961—another cluster—there were three moody travel books about Russia, the U.S.A. and France (the American one was published last year in Michael Kimmage's translation). There were reviews, essays, occasional prose aplenty—but that, as a writer once said, I forget who, is the sort of writing that most writers don't usually think of as writing. And no novels. This was all the more troublesome as Koeppen in 1961 had been the subject of one of those expensive, long-running public transfers of a kind more apt to be associated with European footballers, where they are called "sagas": his publisher, Henry Goverts, went out of business, and Koeppen, with the kind of semi-dignified languid hustle that became his speciality, alerted half a dozen interested publishers, before finally moving to Suhrkamp, where Siegfried Unseld had just lately taken over the reins from the eponymous founder Peter Suhrkamp. Unseld worshipped Koeppen's writing, and soon fell thrall to his difficult personality as well (this is amply documented in their collected correspondence, published by Suhrkamp with the gorgeously, achingly literal title *Ich bitte um ein Wort* (*A Word From You, Please*) in 2006).

Initially all the signs were good: contracts were drawn up and signed, promising with brisk professionalism a play and two novels within two years. In 1962, Koeppen was awarded Germany's most important literary honour, the Büchner Prize. Unseld must have hugged himself for signing a great writer at the top of his game and in his best decade. Over the years Koeppen's backlist was acquired and re-jacketed by Suhrkamp: the post-War trilogy, the travel books, the two early novels from the 30s. And the keenly-awaited new book—the consummation of the deal—that was promised, mooted, announced, described in catalogues and face to face meetings, on occasion even read from. With the passage of time, it also (possibly) morphed identity, not just a moving target but a changing target: it involved Bismarck; it was to do with a masked ball; it was about the folk-hero and trickster Tyl Eulenspiegel; it was called *Into the Dust with all the Enemies of Brandenburg*; it was about the poet Tasso; it was set on a luxury liner. Unseld was in the role of a naturalist who was promised, one after the other, a unicorn, a yeti, a golden goose and a talking horse. And Koeppen? Well, he was always needy, apparently often on the brink of destitution, he had a difficult home life and where his productive morale was concerned he was disturbingly sensitive—but surely he was writing *some*thing, and he was negotiating in good faith?

The noli me tango between publisher/patron and silent, broody author went on for thirty-five years, till Koeppen's death. In the course of it Koeppen took the uncomplaining Unseld—a figure from *Märchen*, if not tragedy or sainthood—for tens, even hundreds of thousands in advances and retainers. A rhythm established itself: Koeppen intimated that he might like to go away somewhere, or that he was tempted by some sublunary offer of work, a journalistic piece for someone or other, something for the radio or television that was of course inopportune but given his circumstances irresistible. Thereupon Unseld would offer him money to go—or to stay—and apply himself to the phantom novel instead: perhaps all it took was an empty apartment in Manhattan. Koeppen would commit himself to a deadline, receive more money, endorse the deadline, be reminded of the deadline (usually it was so that a book might appear in time for the Frankfurt Book Fair of this or that year), miss the deadline, and go quiet, either from calculation or more probably shame. The correspondence, in the lovely term of one of the editors, Alfred Estermann, is an epistolary cosmos with many black holes. Probably there was always some little spark of hope on both sides that something might yet get written, or that Koeppen would finally permit a completed manuscript to emerge into the open. Unseld brought out deluxe editions of tiny opuscula of Koeppen's (and his dearly acquired backlist), while Koeppen's own stock in trade became first his silence, and then the discussion of the silence. German journalists beat a path to his door to ask him about it. It is both agonizing and shameless, coquettishness and torture, as here:

Interviewer: What are you most worried about at the moment?
Koeppen: 'The Ship.'
Interviewer: Is that a book?
Koeppen: 150 pages. But possibly, possibly! A book I've been working on for over a year, and can't seem to get anywhere with."

And so on. (There is a book of these, too.) Surely, you think after reading a few of these, Koeppen has actually taken the hard way out: surely a novel, any novel, is easier than these unendurable questions and stricken answers, this mixture of over-obliging and prevarication. It's the opposite of a trap, or a trap in which the only party really to be caught and to suffer is the party setting it: a trap that bites itself. At its most reduced, artfully configured and psychologically expressive, it takes the form of a title page mocked up by Koeppen and depicted in "*A Word from you, please*": in the middle, the name of author, "Wolfgang Koeppen"; below, a descriptive subtitle, "My Life"; and near the top, the title, one word—though probably not the one Siegfried Unseld was craving for three decades—"No."

The one exception, the single oasis in thirty-five years of literary-commercial desert, the very last of the Sibylline books, is *Jugend* (*Youth*), which was first published in 1976 as number 500 in the iconic Bibliothek Suhrkamp series (there was really no limit to Unseld's generosity and thoughtfulness), when Koeppen turned seventy. "Dear Wolfgang," wrote the gallant Unseld as late as 1 July of that year, "I'm awaiting *Youth* every day, with the sort of intensity with which one only and always waits for youth." This time, for whatever reason, Koeppen didn't disappoint him. Perhaps it was that the book was in 54 separate sections, some of them written long before (he was like a baker, in the German saying, kneading his bread from crumbs)—but I don't want to interrogate its appearance, after wondering so long why nothing else appeared! I heard a story of Koeppen reading aloud from it, in my birthplace, Freiburg: he began, he read for a while, he paused, people left, he had a drink, he carried on, he paused again, more people left. By the end, he had read the whole thing, there was next to no one there, it was midnight, it must have been unforgettable. As Robert Lowell wrote, "genius hums the auditorium dead."

Here, Koeppen's characteristic "No" isn't confined to the title page, but suffused, dissolved throughout the book. What sort of "youth" is it in *Youth*? A second-generation illegitimate child, living alone with his mother who takes in boarders (one of whom makes her pregnant—it's the balloonist/ophthalmologist/anyone-for-tennis figure, one of the more marginal and absurd fathers in literature), and—not sewing—does sewing in the big houses. His experience comprises hunger, boredom, loneliness, punishment, discipline and fear. Have I omitted anything? Towards the end a little chaotic—and largely ineffectual—re-

bellion. His world contrives to be both claustrophobic and ago-
raphobic: little seems to come between him and the steely, striv-
ing, militaristic battery-farm of Wilhelmine Germany with its
twin cults of cruelty and obedience. Whatever he does, which-
ever way he turns, he seems to encounter a main of power, the
Prussian state embodied in teachers, policemen, officers, herring-
sellers, pederasts, sadists, convicts, fraternity medical students,
classmates, heiresses. The young Koeppen feels like one of those
shrunken Beckmann figures who barely fit under an oppressive-
ly low ceiling in a chaotically full room: they are usually the ones
being hanged or scourged or crucified. He goes around barefoot,
in rags, a proto-dropout; the wags in the small town tell him to
see a doctor—who will prescribe a haircut. He's friendless and in
a minority—not just an autodidact, but a self-taught rebel, otherwise one might think the whole thing was fifty years later, in
the 1960s, when rebellion was a sanctioned orthodoxy. When he
goes into the city and witnesses a demonstration, he finds himself, so to speak, snubbed by the proletariat. The sailors don't want
to know either. One might note that not one of the many institutions referred to in these few pages gets off intact: church, par-
liament, university, family, fraternity, army, police, law, hospital,
school, theater, feudal manor or small town; even the local cemetery turns out—small surprise there—to harbor corruption. The
only things that seem to do well in this far from paradisal world
are the snakes, literal and figurative.

But youth as in something to look back on with fondness, as
in salad days and "fair seed-time," to wax nostalgic over? A time of
pleasure, instruction, irresponsibility, secure in the pride and protection of family? Of winsome, attractive, promising growth and
healthy experimentation? Hardly. It is hard to think of another
book not just steeped but cat-drowned in poverty and perspec-
tivelessness, lovelessness, and universal disappointment as this
Youth of Koeppen's—a sort of opposite of *Cider with Rosie*, if you
like. Not that there is anything contrived or showy or larmoyant
about it either. The young Koeppen glimpses the thing the *sou-
brette* is showing him in the window, and bravely toddles upstairs
to claim it. There's no chance, is there, of his mother not taking it

away?! Or later when he picks the lock of the bread-bin and scarfs their bread, or when he wastes the electricity by keeping a light on for himself. The pressure of society and of the history of the period—War, Revolution, Inflation, constant low-level political violence, provincialism, the rise of the Nazi party—has garroted this youth. Nothing is exempt. There is no secret, protected pearl in this book, nothing kept in reserve, no recipe for survival, no self-complacent holy of holies. Sex—except as an expression of power, which he doesn't have—makes no sense to the young Koeppen (after all, how can something that produced him be in any way good?!). He lies chastely beside the young girl in the port of Stettin. Friendship is little short of hubris, an offence to the gods. The young salesman lodger takes him to the cinema for the first time; no wonder he is soon killed in battle. Ditto the communist friend, Lenz. Unforgettable, the son and his mother at night, hibernating: "[wondering] if we should play dead, ignore the summons, draw the curtains to keep out the town. We were a closed society of our own, on occasion stand-offish. We lay in our beds at right angles to each other, not sleeping. We did nothing but listen to the other's breathing; sensing it might stop at any moment, out of fury or fatigue." At a pinch, all there might be is books—and again, not lovingly gone into, but boiled down into one or two lists: books borrowed overnight from the bookshop, and returned in the morning.

Youth ends—this youth does, anyway—before sex and before foreign travel, the point at which the novels begin. It ends at the same place where Knut Hamsun's *Hunger* ends. Tried and found wanting for terrestrial existence. And then, in a final scene, we are given to understand his mother dies—at the age of only forty-four, in 1925. Koeppen is orphaned, and delivered into a profession that isn't really one, that he doesn't want or understand, with which—no pun intended—he can't cope. This character is like a younger, callower version of the adults and young adults who people the novels—just as *Youth*, in the oddest way, offers a kind of concordance to them: military cadets, red swimming trunks, boys' bare legs in shorts, a luminous unapproachable blonde, evening dress, beer (Koeppen disliked beer), gourmandise, Vehmic murders, the cinema, the theater, his horror of a bourgeois public, the railway station and railway porters, the hotel, field-shovels, and many other things besides had a role to play in the novels, and feature in *Youth*. When the Koeppen character is only a little older, he will become Friedrich in *A Sad Affair*, the romantic lead who runs everywhere and gets nowhere; or Philip in *Pigeons on the Grass*, an introverted man of letters in a time of spivs; or the neo-Quixote Keetenheuve, widower and failed MP in *The Hothouse*; or the younger generation of Germans in *Death in Rome*, Adolf Judejahn the Catholic priest, and his cousin Siegfried Pfaffrath, the gay atonal composer. He has nothing to teach them but dissidence, disobedience, disaffection. "Ohne mich," he says in a slogan that—alas for Germany!—didn't become popular till the Sixties: include me out.

One of the points of *Youth* is this all-pervasive ugliness— objectively present, one feels, in the history and project of Prussia, as much as subjective. But one's sense in reading it is overwhelmingly beauty. This is rapturous, sublimely willful, independent-minded, resourceful prose, as Hans Magnus Enzensberger declared, the most beautiful twentieth century German prose. Whether a sentence is a beautifully landscaped torrent going on for several pages or a dumbly insolent "I was Germany's future" or one of Koeppen's patented "or maybe ..." constructions, sidestepping into freedom, it is all scrupulously managed, supple, cadenced, sumptuously lexical, expressive prose.

To set beside this gorgeous, maximalist little piece I chose the very late *Once Upon a Time in Masuria*: a short text spoken by Koeppen over 1990 German television pictures of a return visit by him to the town of Ortelsburg (which after 1945 came into Polish hands as Szczytno). I wanted to offer the reader something plain and uncomplicated and benign, a glass of water to wash down *Youth*.

Michael Hofmann, January 2013

YOUTH

My mother was afraid of snakes. On warm summer days, we walked through the brackish Rosental, the valley regularly flooded by storm tides, to see the house, Ephraimshagen, with its impenetrable whitewashed walls, its Junker-esque avenue of trees, its pilastered doorway of Prusso-Doric plainness, the crumbling, sorry, sandstone blitheness showing the ravages of time as much as the scytheman's hour-glass, the fatuous aspiration to mastery of the main house, its unoverturned hegemony over the peasantry, the old reserve-master-of-horse imposingness of the stables, the black and white striped flagstaff and its pan-German dreams hanging at half-mast; a cock crowed on the dung heap, milk soured in swollen udders, it was a short skip from procreation to slaughter, spirits reeked in the distillery vats, the opened windows yawned in the noonday sun, starched blinds blew white, the foxy red Pomeranian Biedermeier furniture glistened within, the heavy smooth dressers with pillars and gold inlay, the wardrobes with their laurels and garlands, the bedsteads with carved swan necks, the cracked brocade of the armchairs in the drawing room slumbered, the greasy leather chairs in the library stocked with the ranks of the Royal Prussian Army, the hunting calendar, Bismarck's memoirs, and somehow stowed away there and forgotten about Heine's *Buch der Lieder*; the pictures of the dead, their sabers, their pistols, their honour on the walls; a dog trotted over the sand, he didn't know us, a ploughshare rusted, and my mother was speaking, all this is ours, she was screaming, she wanted to din it into me, get it into my thick head, knock it into my heart, that I too bore my share of disappointment and suffering, it was all meant to be my inheritance, because even though my mother was born in the town, in the narrow confines of poverty, she spoke of Ephraimshagen with the bitterness of someone who had been cheated, and I recognized in her small face eaten with fatigue the withered features of my grandmother, saw in my mother's young face my grandmother's wedding picture with the veil like a spider's web draped over her head, daubed by a travelling brush-artist, a despised apprentice, who was given his meals in the kitchen, and who was probably also responsible for the classical ornaments on the walls and ceilings of the house and the frivolous, goose-pimpling figures of the gods basking on fleecy clouds, the ancient seduction, but it remained inexplicable and uncanny, the way he had contrived to suggest something he couldn't have known, the disappointment of love, the false lustre of passion, impending ruin, all in the bride's smile and her eighteen-year-old's garlanded hair, and I saw my grandmother as I had seen her with my infant senses, her face primed for tears with the now swollen and rigid expression of futile scrutiny, as she leaned down over my crib, radiating love and hate, I felt her despair nourishing itself into a mortal growth, because my birth looked like one last and final seal on the decline of the clan, on the loss of honour, on the forfeiture of land and respect; and my mother stared as into paradise along the bumpy clay drive, scabbed by the hooves of the tired shire horses, rutted by the iron-rimmed wheels of the harvest-wagons, cast out expelled from notional security and foolish pride, but I failed to see the Edenic aspect, nothing there attracted me, and on the way home in the evening, midges buzzed and danced over the horrid pools of salt water, my mother heard a rustle in the dried grass, the snakes, she jumped, the treacherous adders of the Rosental, she ran off, the skies loured over the abattoir, thunder and lightning menaced the town, pushed against the famous Friedrich skyline, there were the foals tumbling in the meadow, the lonely men gazing sadly at the moon, the boats at anchor sleeping with their masts inclining dreamily to Africa, the roofs and steeples of St. Nikolai, St. Jakob, and St. Mary, oppressing the faithful with their bulk, their red brick stacked against the unattainable heaven, resembling crazed hypertrophic fortresses, grown old in desert, wilderness and swamp, and in the churches lay abandoned the empty naves, prayerless halls behind locked doors, withdrawn from the grace of confession and absolution, the unadorned Protestant altars, the pulpits of hectoring preachers, the lost rebellion of buried consciences, while all around the streets smelled complacently of smoked eel, of fried potato and fish suppers, bacon and bran bread, buckwheat kasha and lumpy groats, of respectability, sly head-down ordinariness, domestic stupidity and vindictiveness, of the decaying memory of the poor heroes of the war, of the conserved beautiful corpse of the empire, the Pasewalk cuirassier stabbed in the back picked out in red thread on kitchen linens, of the dueling blood of students dribbling over the stinking fraternity tunic into the sawdust of pubs, of the blood of those murdered by rabid nationalists and lowered into the peat bog, carried down to the Huns' graves, of the blood of girls in their hidden undies stuffed down the back of the sofa, of asepsis and pus, of the anatomy of clinics, the sweat of patients, the horror of the dying, the fear of the examinee and the guilty innocents at the mercy of the prison-warders, of the madness of the deranged inmates of the institution on the other side of the tracks and the jokes that were made about them, of the rotted flowers of the cemeteries and the death that everyone carries in his chest, of the decaying puddle of moat water and effluent, of the panting of lovers under the bushes in the rowboats of summer, of the vanity of professors, the dead hearts of officials, the frowst of the laws, and then the poverty of the Lange Reihe and the indurated humiliation of the gray school, how I hated the city and wished it consigned to the snakes, a glib adder round every post that bore a roof or supported a bed and the deep sleep of the just.

In the beginning, God created Heaven and Earth, and Maria (who liked to go by Mary) thought He had also created her town and sunned Himself in it, even if it remained a mystery how He could ignore so much misfortune, unless it were that the unfortunates were bad seed and were banished from His sight, as many people claimed, but that wasn't true, or not entirely true, and that left God looking down rather foolishly, which was fine by Maria, because she too wanted to see that all was good, because she loved the town, and set it ahead of all others—which she had never seen.

Maria walks down the Lange Strasse with Bismarck, she walks Bismarck at the time people like to go for their constitutionals, between five and six, when everyone likes to walk and show themselves off, order is kept up rigidly, and morality is under assault but only in a way approved of by morality, Maria is grateful to be out walking with Bismarck, who doesn't belong to her, but who obeys her, so that she lives as it were in his reflected glory, and she loves Bismarck and is proud of him.

She doesn't mind how constricted circumstances are, how limited freedom, how rigid the rules. A scion of the Imperial family is visiting the town. The District President, the Lord Mayor, the Chief of Police, the commanding officer of the local garrison, the Chancellor of the University, all respectfully bow the neck. The scion is gracious, the scion says whatever he had been expected to say. Morning coats, top hats, uniforms, and plumed helmets and the full fig of students take over the Lange Strasse. Maria has no instinct for the devils that surround her and dominate the scene, because these devils are old and gray and the only reason they have invented the colorful ceremony of the parade is to divert attention from themselves and live out their gray vampire days in gray apartments of luxury and incest. Laughter, Maria hears it or she contrives to ignore it, or she doesn't know what it means, scrapes out of the windows, laughter at all those who are down below, to make them stay there. From all the cellar windows breathes an agricultural past, agricultural greed, the never forgotten loan on the reverted field, the doubt growing whether they would prosper in the town, and for how long. Wronker's vinegar and mustard works sours the streets, sours the road to the gray convent, to the old folks' home, to the gray convent school for middle class children. Fräulein Wronker's carriage and pair goes jouncing over the cobblestones. A doctor of German and Roman Laws walks the Wall, and thinks what a match Fräulein Wronker would make. The vinegar brewer's daughter will make a wife for a lawyer or notary, even a public prosecutor or judge. She will run her own household, indistinguishable from the households of other silly hens who have become judges' wives. Fräulein Wronker will even agree to being humiliated on account of her origins in manufacturing. Maria is jealous of Fräulein Wronker's horses and prospects, but at the same time she quite genuinely despises her and thinks, I wouldn't trade places with you, no thanks. At Susemihl's there's a smell of marinades. Burgundy and Bordeaux by the barrel and the bottle. Lager ripens. Bruggemann's textile house has the gluey smell of starch. At Bugenhagen's bookshop, learning makes a crisp, papery sound like a comb passing through hair. A dry sound, an occasional spark.

All the windows watch Maria, lizard's eyes in a murky pool. Maria is nineteen and blooming. Bismarck pulls her forward like one of Borsig's new locomotives. Bismarck is big and strong, he protects her, his muscles twitch and roll under his short fur, his mouth makes menaces, his eyes are loyal. Maria knows the colors of all the fraternities and clubs. It's the whole world wandering down the Lange Strasse, because all those in colored caps with sashes across their breasts and dueling scars on their faces are there, they are society, they are the props of throne and altar, they are the German Empire. They stand out, nothing counts but them. The young clerk at Susemihl's blushes when Maria passes, a silly man, a herring-tamer, even as he dips his wooden tongs into the scale-glittering brine to pull out salt fishes for her and her mother's lunch. She has to beg the cobbler to fix the soles on her worn shoes, one last, final time. The cobbler is not a man, or at least not a human being. He is a function, he makes and repairs shoes, because society, that sacrosanct institution to which Maria does not belong, but of which she considers herself a part, abhors bare feet. The cobbler's fingers are nimble, but they don't matter. He shuts up shop, only to retire into the facelessness of the common people. The lieutenant stands in front of his serge-clad men on the parade ground, in front of the red jerry-built barracks. Even the Borussian in his white cap is careful to greet him first. Maria is cheerful. She would have felt sorry for the cobbler as for a beggar; if he had been thrown out of his shop or room for owing the rent, she would have been moved by his misfortune, just as her own and her mother's always brought her to tears. Maria is cheerful, but the cobbler's trade and craft are impossible. As Maria is poor, she worships property. As she feels *déclassée*, she worships the ruling class. The poor man thinks about bread. The rich man is busy with flowers. Maria has no idea how people go about

acquiring property. With bandaged eyes (the blinkers of foolish-
ness are tied around her), she attempts the magic trick of being a
young lady without money or position. Anyone who works, who
provides a service, who follows a trade or profession, is excluded
from the ladies' world, and so Maria and her mother live by letting out rooms to students and the odd tutor. That was how she
came by Bismarck, who belongs to a gentleman who has the *venia
legendi* of ophthalmology. In gentle zephyrs he likes to orbit the
towers of the town in a lighter-than-air balloon. How beautiful is
the hour of the *passaggiata* on the Lange Strasse, in summer light
clarified by the sea breeze or the cheery gaslights or the Christmas
displays in the shop windows.

It wasn't nice, what people said and the way they said it, and the
worst of it was that she had to listen hard to snap up something
she didn't want to know but that it was important to know, the
world was changing, no new shore hove into view, it was the old
country, the native valley, a female hell, mother's corn drunks,
witches' brew, pathless forests, and on the dark tall trees, a sign-
post, *juniperus sabrina*, like the ones in the botanical gardens
put there by Professor Pryl, sticky whisperings, mocking giggles,
twitching curtains, an accommodation with one's horror; it must
have seemed to her as though she had been deaf thus far, blind,
unable to read, to taste, to feel, to smell, because everywhere there
were the terrible secrets, hidden behind perfectly ordinary things,
or anyway behind allegories or symbols that she had failed to notice and hadn't correctly interpreted, till everyone was forced to
notice and interpret them, and her friend, the piano teacher's
daughter Käte Kasch, so alert and quick on the uptake, of whom
it was said, she's no friend for you, you mustn't go around with
her, she's got no self-respect, you know where that leads, and yes,
people had indeed known, it led where, to Käte Kasch being more
savvy, and she affirmed your fear, and then along came the old
wives' recipes, the teas, the pine needle distillates, the claret from
Susemihl's store, warmed with saffron, cloves and cinnamon, al-
ternating baths for the feet and arms, hot and cold showers for the
hands, and then the smelly and in their dirty way clean rooms of

those women, their red potash hands, their rinsed washerwomen's hands, their shameless sisters' hands and the certainty that she was lost, branded on the altar of the cruel goddess Morality, subject to the blind philoprogenitive goddess Nature, and her disgust at those hands, and her disgust at those cold dismissive eyes, her fear of the blunt and pointy tools, her revulsion against her own body, her beating against her own body, the frantic dance steps, and the skipping rope and the running up and downstairs, where it would have taken a leap off the high tower of St. Nikolai's church to have made a difference, which was something she probably considered as well.

Pommerland ist abgebrannt, not yet, not for a long time or maybe soon, Pommerland is getting ready for the fire, the fuse is laid, the tinder is secreted, sulfur is scattered and pitch, it swells and molders and grows, the seed is burning in you too, you don't know it, you don't realize it, you don't think, how could you, no one notices anything, no one thinks, even university professors don't notice and don't think, any more than the District President, Count Bär-Bärenhof, he sees the fire glow and sniffs a new dawn, or the garrison-commander, Major von Schulz, apart from the Almighty all he fears is retirement and endless days alone with his wife, without glamour and subordination, and he has no fear that he will be promoted to colonel and hero and corpse in a hero's grave in ancestral enemy soil, there are no trees and no ladybirds on the Hunnenstrasse, balloons fly around, who wouldn't want to go up in one too, green field white beach field gray the land, undefended the coast, toiling and moiling the sea, the fog establishes its empire, the red brick steeples oppose the clear or cloudy skies, churches like brooding hens, standing-stones in ploughed fields, never slain giants, buckwheat opposes the storm, buckwheat gruel and milk spills over the edge of the bowl, crows by day, owls at night.

Like the poor shaven skulls of boys, the stones of the Hunnenstrasse bunch together, wet or dry, warm or cold, I feel the roundness and hardness of the stones through the soles of my worn out school shoes, through the horrid scratchy wool socks, through my torn summer socks, smooth and cool under bare feet, it's a bumpy street, it presses itself into my skin, I haven't been toughened up yet, that's all ahead of me.

The road goes down to the port, I hope, I fear, it goes out into the world, away from the Hunnenstrasse, straight to China, where they are yellow-skinned and wear long black pigtails, my Kaiser will punish them, my Kaiser owns the ships in the port, the ferry to Wiek in summer, the Sunday pleasure-steamer to Rügen, the heavy barges full of coal, sugar beets, potatoes, corn, the herring- and flounder-boats with their rust-red sails, the swift *Aviso*, a panther against the heathen, the sea-gray fog-gray victory-gray torpedo boat patrol, it often rains, water stuffs the gutters, streams burble into the sea, sweeping with them proud armadas of trash.

Wagon wheels have iron rims; they clatter like gun carriages, like the cannonballs of the old Swedes battering the town walls, rolling and grumbling like thunder, the houses on the Hunnenstrasse tremble, cower, are used to it, old whitewash gone gray, rickety facades, steep gables, sooty chimneys, acrid smoke of peat.

Flanking the low windows are heavy shutters of stout wood, wind traps, clattering against the walls and windows in a gale. The inhabitants pull them to, seagoing or landlubbing populus, tie up the shutters like sails on a boat on the verge of going down. In the evening, they bang their doors shut, nail themselves in, batten down the hatches, sit proud and fearful in the possession they're helping to secure, only criminals are abroad at night. The policeman's saber jangles against the cobbles, sparks fly, martial the eye of the trusty watchman, his beard bristles over his foolish mouth, fashion is set by the tigers or the Kaiser, wind-chapped, schnapps-reddened jowls wobble over the blue uniform collar, the body is a friendly sack of oats. That body, that sack! The bayonet is fixed, on the exercise yard the cadet learns the art of bayonetting, a sack stands in for a body, a proper man wants nothing better than to fight for king and country, preferably in hand-to-hand combat. Sometimes in his dreams, the policeman is the sack. Other than that, everything is as it should be. The gaslight, gloomy black wrought-iron raven, screwed on to the house like a gallows. The old pump of moldering wood hasn't been stolen, the curb not soiled. There's no dodgy or doggy business in the precinct. The King's citizens, the Kaiser's subjects, the cobbler's ball covered over, the tailor's table as shiny as the seat of your pants. In Schütter's greengrocer's cellar, potatoes are germinating, with dark longings wrapping pale arms around the turnips.

Under the schoolmaster's rooms there are strange hauntings, and so he tenaciously clings to his idea of the seriousness of life, where sinful childishness is to be eradicated root and branch, by the cane. The captain's widow is awash under her billowing featherbed. What's keeping the captain? Oh, in the silver frame on the sideboard, leaning against a little ornamental pillar, the hand that held the tiller on a crocheted place mat, with the imaginary addition of Chinese typhoons and yellow fire-spitting dragons. And the sexton of St. Nikolai is a very serious gentleman, black tailcoat, black tie, black pastoral hat. Is his handkerchief black as well, does he brandish it blackly against the heavens? Will the black sky respond? The sexton looks up the tall steeple. The weather is coming from the sea. The Lord's lightning will strike anyone rash enough to raise his head.

St. Nikolai casts its heavy Lutheran shadow across the Hunnenstrasse. The drunks will be along later. The Hunnenstrasse isn't named for the Huns, the Huns will attack the street, only not on horseback, they will pass along it in triumph, they are the victors on foot, there they are, they are happy people laughing and singing and treading on the coarse stones, on special days in boots and spurs, they look earnest and a little terrifying with their twirled moustaches, with their whippy sticks they strike and stroke and prod the cracked lintels, the ancient walls, the gnomish faces of the houses, they peer in at the ground floor windows, rootle around among the beds, the old house altar of conception and birth and death, rummage among the legs of the laundry tables, the reed-grown watering cans, the fast or slow or stopped clocks with their stalled or swinging pendulums, the heads of dead stags, the portraits of distinguished gentlemen behind glass or in oils, the damaged knickknacks on the walnut cabinet, the sugar plum fairies teetering in front of shells where you can listen to the hiss of the sea, the heavy castle gates, the worn the stripped the made-ready clothes, the empty or full cribs, the Huns desire, they demand booty, they sing a song *o filia hospitales*, Cherusci, Vandals, Teutons, Cimbri, green blue red yellow caps and the black masks of the fresh bandages after the bloody duel, the sharp slashes of the scarring sabers, a high whine in the air, frozen over the plastered faces, pain drenches the skin, drenches my skin, penetrates my flesh, tears a gaping slash into it, the bare wound burns like fire and stings like a nettle, the grievous whiff of disinfectant billows through the street, the bright otherworldly smell of old anatomy intoxicates me, a rainbow precedes me in green red blue yellow spectrum, its dome is over the university, it clears the monument to the founder, sinks in the pubs, I look up and down at the beautiful rainbow, high in the lofty garret, tiny in the grubby gutter, and the people exist as well, my mother says so, fishwives pushing their carts, fishwhores with whorefish, sodden witches in layers of black hessian, the marmalade cat eats the green bones, licks its lips, a rosy tongue, fresh flounders, russet brown slippery-smooth, fight against their fate, monsters of the deep exhibited by the crateload, herring, herring, white lard clarifies in the crusty frying pan, the reek goes up your nose, hangs in the street, lunch smells, thanksgiving, come O Jesu, here comes the Reverend with his Scriptural tags, the birds and the lilies of the valley, Jesus and the Reverend forgive sinners, the others are different, people who have a job, a post, a trade or craft, and finally the day laborers, people who count for nothing and carry loads and clear away filth, then the middle class, which is respectable, thus my mother, I dutifully doff my cap, wave his Majesty's ship on the crest, bow low to the stout gaunt ruddy pale small big rowdy quiet always worthy always offended men who help who provide who have credit who do not provide who do not have credit, men with prejudices who cause others to starve and be destroyed, my mother is afraid of snakes, but she is also afraid of hands, big hands hairy hands fat bony ringed red hands, men she has to beg, the grocer Susemihl please a ball a globe of all his wares, a marbled waistcoat a heavy dangling golden chain, a watch he likes to consult, a watch with the grim reaper Death on it, a pleasantly

chilling ringing of the hours, and Kleuke, who deals in solid fu-
els, an evil winter god, the guardian of the fire, sits in the cozy
hell of his coal-black office, a steamer of the Hamburg-Amer-
ica Line slices the blue waves over his head, a coal miner with
his miner's lamp on his miner's helmet shows off a couple of bri-
quettes the way Moses might have showed off the tablets with
the Commandments, the sheepish coughings of Fietze the land-
lord demanding tribute, the rent for the garret, but all of them in
terms of the respect one owes them are classed below the Doctor
and the Professor and the Reverend, but not nearly as high as the
landowners who stayed on in paradise after we were expelled, still
hugging the heights of the flat land, my mother avers, the landowners belong to the officer class, the real great ones, long blue
coats, not a speck of dust, high red collar, no crease, straight cap
brim or glittering metal helm, a fish that the fishwives wouldn't
call out or throw on their scales, the Hunnenstrasse derives its
name from dogs, from the *plattdeutsch* way they pronounce dogs
in Pomerania, from hounds.

Feetenbrink's concert hall was a palace on the Hunnenstrasse, sin-
gle-storey like the rest of the buildings, but a long façade, lit up at
night, the way ordinary houses were only on the Kaiser's birthday,
with laurel and quarrel and victory candles in the windows. The
concert hall was both the glory and the shame of the Hunnenstrasse, it bestowed on it both light and shade. Everyone saw who
went to Feetenbrink's. Not just the old women squatting behind
the mirrors at their windows, pushing them out over the street
like periscopes or octopus' eyes and registering any occurrence,
storing their data, ready at any time to spit them out again, pal-
lidly dismayed, envy-green, early electronic brains.

The carriages of the landowners draw up, I admire them, I
prowl around them, slack-jawed, shimmer of lacquer, sheen of
leather, brown-black grease slathers the axle-joints and the thole-
pins, the horses' coats darken and steam and shine, the groom,
old queen's cuirassier, extends an invisible standard when he
speaks or hears the name of Pasewalk, the town where he served,
where he was ground up small, where he wore tight white pants,

he looks like the trumpeter of Thionville, like the attack on Mars-la-Tour, and all I can think of is Pasewalk fritters, sweet, light and greasy like sultry sugared air, my mother is mad for them, nothing bad could come from Pasewalk, the groom takes the reins that are kindly tossed him, he knows how to give satisfaction, Captain of Horse, Captain, Colonel Baron von and zu Kluttegrutt, the visitor, honor the visitor, a broad back, he wheezes up the three stone steps, fills the doorway, rolls into the building, in winter a fur dangles, snow-wet, forest-chilled, in summer some light fabric is drawn across his shoulders and bum, Nanking, wedged into his crutch, stretched heavily and sweatily over the plump field-walker's thighs, cigar smoke remains behind, a whiff of gunsmoke, the groom takes off the horses' harnesses, rubs them down and covers them with a woolen cloth, takes them by the bridle, leads them patiently to the stable, I go in after them, I curry favor with the horses and their groom, the horses are friendly, they have gentle dark eyes, the groom drives me out of the stable cursing, in the concert hall they start playing the piano, laughter gurgles, snatches of broken words stumble across the street.

The curtain is pushed aside, I'm standing outside the house, taking everything in, a woman appears in the window, raps on the pane, she's rapping to me, I was expecting it, a secret shiver passes through me, I think she's tapping with her golden ring, she's tapping with her green stone, she's holding something in her hand, she's beckoning to me, I can't see what she's holding out to me, but it's endlessly desirable, her hand is beckoning, I'm scared, I look around for support, someone to go with me, or for enemies who could stand in my way, I'm tempted, I can't refuse, I climb up the three stone steps, I tiptoe through the open door, I'm the fat landowner in fur or Nanking, I inhale beer and smoke, now the piano sounds louder, the laughter brighter, the words sharper, the steps lead straight up, a red stair-carpet covers them, the red carpet shows the way, I make an effort, I crawl higher, the carpet is rough, the carpet scrapes my palms and my knees, on the first floor landing is the coconut, an alabaster lamp shaded by palm leaves, the passage is shady, it's warm and bubbling, it's as warm as the stables, but the beast that lives here is no horse, it tickles my nose like the smell of Dehmel's barbershop, pungent soap, pungent flowers drying in the family album among relatives among the dead among people that someone knew and whose photographic image one received and preserved and can't imagine anymore, and other flowers that are kept too long in the same water in their vase, a disgusting smell of dried blood, the door is opened a crack, a stab of light, cloth slides back, an arm sleeved in white, the woman pulls me in to her, it was her knocking on the window, she was beckoning me in, she wears a robe the like of which I have never seen, the robe of a queen or a fairy, it seems to be made up entirely of lace and feathers, a colorful bird is strutting about in front of me, fluttering, flapping its wings, it breaks free of the room, the woman's hair shines like a blond sun, Rapunzel but with a harlequin's face, smudged in red and white, the eyes the blue of tar puddles, the brows anthracite black, her bosom is like a bed with two plump pillows, a shelter in chill nights, her voice cheers, a singer, a nightingale, she gives me what she showed me at the window, a rider on a horse, both horse and rider are made of wood, the horse is white and black, the rider is white and red, I love both horse and rider, I will never let them out of my hand, I press them to my chest and I start to cry, my mother is upset with me.

She heard him going up the stairs, she heard his inhibited, guilty footfall, he had been over in Feetenbrink's, and to her it was as if a man had been over there, her husband or her son in due time, grown up and to her chagrin a layabout, dishonest, disreputable, hanging around with girls, there was no end to the disgrace, and if she had come through, reflective, as people said, improved, after she had suffered her misfortune, well, he might yet go before the court, borstal, prison, barred windows that one could see from the Kastanienwall, walking and with a hefty shudder, his father had played tennis once on the square under the Kastanienwall, before the tall gray wall, and she had watched him from above, from up on the dyke, how he, the father, had gone leaping over the red sand of the tennis court, in long white trousers, an elastic loop pulling them down over his shoes, a white panama hat on his head, running up to the net, chasing after the ball, and she had not been permitted to set foot on the court, because it was reserved for Members of the University Tennis Club, and perhaps a prisoner, a thief or murderer had been able to see her over the prison wall, through the tiny barred window of his cell, on the dyke under the chestnut trees, and envied her watching the man playing tennis; she had to be strict with him, the boy she had had with that young man, it was her duty as a Christian, and she sensed, she could see it through the door, that he had been given something, he was clasping it to himself in his small dirty paw, he was waiting, trembling already that he would have to give it up, and he hesitated by the door and didn't want to come in and be parted from his present, he hugged it close the gift from one of those singers, those travelling, homeless music hall singers thrown out of their parents' homes, whom, like all the world, she despised and secretly also envied, because who could say, maybe those creatures were free, maybe they were able to live happily beyond the border of decency and righteousness, which for her was the same as the land of poverty, while these ladies, these barflies, had left decency behind, and perhaps poverty as well, and were now oppressing (with caprice, rejection, two-timing and exploitation, oppressing) their oppressors, but to think like that was terribly dangerous, she mustn't think like that, this frontier where she had been made to stand once before, had to remain drawn otherwise she would be lost in her town. She heard his footfall, she heard his quiet loitering outside the door, and while she listened and felt angry with him and yet proud of him, his step on the old creaking stairs, his waiting on the loose board at the top of the steps, she also heard other steps, the brisk, indifferent clop of the undertakers who had carried her mother downstairs, her mother who had seen the tragedy in everything and had always bewailed it and had never understood it or perhaps wanted to understand it, that this whole fall had been a result of that first original fall, her daring leap to freedom, blindly and without even minding about freedom, she didn't use the word, she didn't know it in its unconditional, its absolute sense, and if someone had said it to her, called it out to her at the moment of departure, about to jump and indeed jumping clear of her marriage, of the family, of ancestry, of the ownership of an estate with all its animals, its fields and trees, the rebellion implicit in the word might only have alarmed her, and perhaps she would have thought better of everything, of leaving, of leaping, because it had been dinned into her, and she wasn't one to doubt the word of any preacherman, that rebellion was a sin, it was the devil's work, and she was still in agreement with the preacher, and she was obedient to authority, and conformed to the morality that oppressed her; but no one had come to speak to her of freedom and to alarm her, she ran blindly, thinking she was running from one house to another, brighter house, a new home that she never reached and that could never have been found anyway on the path down which she was blindly, ignorantly running, or not by her at any rate, and so she saw herself all her life as the victim of misfortune, battered by destiny, poor and finally old woman, with Care at her bedside, another poor old woman, almost her mirror image, and she handed down her sense of misfortune and victimhood, of Job-like sufferings, another phrase she had picked up from a sermon, because it so richly and beautifully evoked misfortune, handed that on down to her, the daughter, who now could hear her own son breathing behind the door, and took this for a sign that affirmed the hereditary transmitted misfortune, and pressed on it the final seal of exclusion from the society of the good. And the child for its part saw not just the closed door in front of him, the brown painted wood, the black wrought iron knocker to which he dared not raise his hand, the child saw the coffin being carried out, the face of his grandmother leaning down over him in his crib or the old Moses basket or chest of drawers in which he had been laid, dangling there for hours, like a moon, a small pale moon with moon craters and moon lakes and moon shadows, moonlight from the lamp or through the window, very clear, very distinct, as on a map of the moon, long before the child ever saw the real moon up in the heavens, serious, beaten, also friendly, but friendly in a beaten sort of way, sometimes veiled in thoughts of murder and then bathed in tears, blaming him, the child sensed it, but he did not cry, he stared back, didn't fight, didn't yield either, they understood each other. The moon spoke to him, and the child answered. All without words.

She threw the earth down on the coffin, on the woman who lay in the coffin, and as she buried her mother, she looked over the green hedges of the cemetery at the town's familiar steeples, which did not oppress her, from which she did not desire to flee, the tall red roofs of St. Maria, St. Jakob, and St. Nikolai, and she identified right away the gasworks with its black gasometers, close to the cemetery, just behind the last of the hedges, she smelled the gas and saw it pouring through a tube, filling the tube, the tube swelling, a fat, rearing snake that ran into the balloon, filling it, which then, yellow, sun-like, hung in its net over the gondola, tugging at its guy-ropes, and finally climbed high over the roofs and steeples, floated away across the land and the river, also over the cemetery until it finally slowly went out to sea. And she had remained down below, running in consternation after the false sun, running through streets and alleyways, wandering over the dyke, under the old shadow-giving, privacy-giving trees, and the shout in her did not grow loud, she stifled it, it choked her, because she was certain now that she would have to whisper all her life, she couldn't bear it, couldn't stand it, that this was her life, she refused, she beat herself, but it could not be shaken off, this thing that had been committed to her, the horror that was in her, that grew in her belly and went with her and stayed with her, and would stay with her, and all over the town, on every street, in every window, in every room, there were eyes measuring her, fingers pointing at her, mouths vilifying her.

Our clothes were wet with rain. The storm had passed and was grumbling again. We were running with sweat under our sodden clothes. The plants were steaming in the damp heavy air. The trees wept. The cemetery gardener led us to the tomb in one of his imposing buildings in the beautiful old graveyard. The gardener's buildings had entrances of Greek columns, that held up the pointed gables in front of the roof; but they were very low houses in which the dead dwelt, the prosperous dead, the dead who alive had been wealthy and who were not now given to the common earth, not bundled down into the basement, not into the moldy hole of a common-or-garden grave, not under roots or shared among busy industrious hungry worms. The dead in the mausoleums came from the old vampiric lineages of the town, the mighty circle of patrician mummies who had always kept up a worthy home for their dear departed, exclusively, and in fear but also in hope. The house we entered was uninhabited, no dead person was resting on a bier, no corpse summoned to lunch. Perhaps the family that under this roof had mourned or applauded humanist culture had died out or become impoverished or disgraced, or they had lost their grip, their firm faith in themselves, the self-evidence of ownership, the priggishness of entitlement or had merely lost respect through good fortune, and become indifferent to their ancestors. And no one knew now where the dead man was, his bones that must have dwelt here well covered, no one knew or wanted to know, the cemetery gardener was in on the conspiracy, perhaps they had thrown out their forefather's bones at dead of night on the cemetery rubbish, the dead man was exmitted, his check hadn't been honored, his rent not kept up to date. The town never thought twice about repossessing a debtor's bed. But chairs had been left behind in the mausoleum, seats for mourners, thrones for happy heirs, gilt chairs, but the gold had flaked off, we saw the crumbling worm-chewed wood like spoiled maggot-infested flour, and over it the velvet that had once been royal purple was now disintegrating in dirty patches, striations and scrapes over mucus yellow clouds of rotting wool. We were so exhausted by death and corpse agony and leave-taking and scourging and the view into the open grave and the roped descent of the coffin that we no longer cried, only, lashed by the rain became the cemetery gardener's impassive boulders: the orphaned death chairs suited us, we found them soft, and sank into sleep in their moldering cushions, rested in the lapsed grave of a respected man, the dead man had made way for us, and socially boosted us, in the silent storm the moldy boat was deceptive, and we sought peace in strife. The gravedigger and his guests had nothing with which to drink a toast to one another. The gravedigger looked expectantly at the child in blue and white striped cotton, with his starched sailor's collar. Ivy will grow on the grave, and lots of evergreen plants emblematic of everlasting life, the stern aromatic rustling smells of the box hedges will prettify mourning, the passing bell tolls, the foghorn booms, there is no help for the sinking boat, the too-whit of the screech owl affrights the midnight, the Aeolian harp in the garden is the judge's foe and the child's astonishment, over and over again.

Very personal memories connect me to Bismarck. We resemble one another. Bismarck wept, he threw himself down on the sofa, the heavy body, I picture it to myself, the white antimacassar, the sofa cushions stitched with loving hand, the sofa tassels combed with doting hand, and Bismarck wailing. Not me. They had drummed it into me as a child, and invoking the name of Bismarck or of some Prussian king: A grown man doesn't cry. So I only cry when I am Bismarck. I got to know him early on, Bismarck was on the sewing machine or next to the sewing machine, on which my mother was patching the bed linen for one of those Pomeranian nobleman's estates, Lossin or Wunkenhagen or Demeritz, and Bismarck was cast in bronze, he was wearing boots that were one hundred per cent bronze, he was holding a bronze saber in his bronze hand, and on his bronze head perched an eagle, also bronze. On his bronze helmet. The figure looked as though it meant to intimidate me. Bismarck weighed a lot, and I wasn't able to lift him at the time, but if a grown man had got hold of him, then he would have been able to kill another man with him. The lord of Lossin or Wunkenhagen or the lord of Demeritz didn't do that. He had a shovel that he used to kill people with. But the lords of Lossin or Wunkenhagen or Demeritz didn't use their shovels either. They used their staff. They had always had staffs on Lossin or Wunkenhagen or Demeritz, and even after the suspension of feudalism and the abolition of the authority of the lord of the manor, people continued to be born on Lossin or Wunkenhagen or Demeritz or people were brought to those places for the purpose of killing others. That estate called Lossin, or Wunkenhagen or Demeritz, it had belonged to my mother, or to my mother's mother, I was never quite sure, I had heard it too many times and it was told me or not told me in too many different ways, and it was true that my mother did sewing work on those estates, but she couldn't sew, even though people seemed to take it for granted that a woman in her position would be able to sew, and so she stitched the sheets of rough peasant linen for a mark a day, and the great perk was that she was able to take me with her. And so I sat under the sewing machine, and watched my mother's feet as they operated the treadle, and the sheets passed under the needle of the sewing machine, and they rose and fell and rose and fell before my eyes like the curtains of a stage on which Bismarck appeared, or where an actor playing the part of Bismarck stepped forward to thank the audience for their applause. Cast in bronze, and torchlight processions of students passed out of the town to the Bismarck Tower, where they dropped their burning torches at the feet of the monument, and Bismarck, he too in bronze, stood firm-footed on his pedestal, firm-faced, firm-expressioned, firm-fleshed, all bronze, in the flickering torchlight in the darkness, and nothing could go wrong again. At that time, sitting under the sewing machine next to my mother's feet moving the wheel, it never occurred to me that the bedsheets that rose and fell and flickered before my eyes, might have been likened to funeral shrouds or to the white flags of defeat.

What had happened? Something had happened, it hadn't happened at home, it would never have occurred to his mother, she would not have wanted that, and they had never owned such a book anyway, but his mother was desperate, everyone said she was desperate, people expected her to be desperate, perhaps she eventually became desperate, and since there was a war on, she had more to be desperate about, or maybe less, families adjusted to the prospect of death, a shining happy death, it was only the enemy for whom death came as painful extinction, Germany was proving itself, the Kaiser said there were no more political parties, the populous was led to the trenches and a shining future, and all were ready to hold together and forgive old sins, inasmuch as such Christian and patriotic behavior remained in God-given bounds, and didn't imperil the status quo or public morality; so the gentlemen had invited her to a war-soup, and the book had turned up somewhere, in one of those estate libraries that looked out onto the big house, the avenue of limes, the sodden willows, the nightshade-green potato fields, the horizon of beet fields, some grain, the broad-leaved wood, a rune-stone, black and white cows, fog off the Baltic, there, beside the regimental history, beside the hunting calendar, the fleet calendar, the colonial calendar, beside Bismarck's memoirs, unread or half-read and un-understood, where he had cried, beside the gun-cupboard, in front of the green baize, and someone had remembered that someone or other had used to be a general one time, a dead general now, maybe Bismarck, but even a dead general, maybe Bismarck, enjoyed the highest esteem, had comrades beyond the grave, and the fellow to whom this occurred, Herr von Lossin or Herr von Wunkenhagen or von Demeritz, knew that he had connections, and that it was against the regulations, corrupt and not at all nice, but for all that in wartime and in memory of the old dead general, Bismarck maybe, a good work, it was a matter of lowering a dangerous branch of the family tree, on account of the sin, but perhaps also to give it a chance to recover itself and be accepted again, on account of the albeit rotten trunk, both, and he had taken the volume down from the shelf, an indispensable source of information for everyone in popular form, our army, our navy, the binding was massive, the book was nailed together, God with us in gold on black ground and the Prussian eagle black on gold ground and then himself on the very first three-colour etching, no not him, so much as him the way he ought to look had ought to look and now no longer looked, grizzled and maybe sunk, his Majesty's ship of the line, *Kaiser Wilhelm II*, wave-rinsed, foam-crested, bow-armored, gold-betressed, eagle-mounted, the one and only terrifying man of war, and then next came the order, the bacon in the trap, the bacon that the boy didn't eat, the bacon and the trap that kidnapped it, and they said to his mother, that boy is a millstone round your neck, and is getting in your way now it's wartime, he stops you coming out to our estates to sew, to fix our

sheets, sometimes he sits with you at table, sometimes not, one
mark per sewing day, with free board, albeit in the kitchen, and
you can make something of your bastard if he behaves himself,
but they didn't expect good behavior, they winked at one another,
why, he could become a general, a field-marshal, maybe the next
Bismarck, they kidded, and they smacked their thighs, and his
mother whispered, or at least professor, then they thought of the
leaflets, the gossip, the figure of fun in his morning coat, with his
black broad-brimmed hat, his umbrella parked next to him, redolent of the Paulskirche, while she pictured him in English flan-
nel, an aeronaut in the peaked cap of the Kaiser's yacht club, the
branch was rotten, they didn't choke on their laughter, but nothing was impossible to God, Pastor Wullwebe said so in his ser-
mons or was it the actual Bible itself, and morality and behavior
were certain, they grew serious and looked into a grail, the place
of purification, and they took back the beer-nail-studded book,
and checked the address

the application to the charitable institution is to be addressed to
the Royal Prussian Army's Department of Education and Culture, in Berlin Wilhelmstrasse, 82-85, and Herr von Demeritz,
or von Lossin, or Herr von Wunkenhagen liked travelling to the
royal capital and sin city, full of memories, certain of future prospects, a will and a way, but whose will and whose way, retired
Major, retired Master of Horse, Lieutenant Colonel on second-
ment, released back to their estates, Home Guard in old splendor
and majesty, curious war, no Uhlan patrols, the landowner took
with him a rabbit he'd shot, Berlin was starving, so people said,
and took with him a smoked goose breast, and improperly and a
little grotesquely, he took with him a sack of flour from his own
fields, hidden in a wicker basket, he ran into compeers, he was
a member of the upper house, well-liked, in the *cabinet particu-
lier* at Hiller's you could still get lobster and Chablis, but worry
was there at the feast, had a fine tongue, the man in Command
of the Marks lowered his head, almost choked, a strange scratch-
ing gagging fear in his throat, something was going agley, dyed
in wool conservatives were at daggers drawn, almost distrusted

themselves, thinking of their cousins in Petersburg, small conso-
lation, in the Wilhelmstrasse gazing out of the Classico-Prussian
windows were Bismarck, von Caprivi, Chlodwig Baron zu Ho-
henlohe-Schillingsfürst, Bernhard Baron von Bülow, a great tren-
cherman, Bethmann-Hollweg, an ascete and official in uniform,
Moltke the elder sent his regards, his cap brim set straight across
his thoughtful brow, his nephew Helmuth had already been ca-
shiered, the emergency was at hand, expectedly, unexpectedly, Alfred Count von Schlieffen had relocated to a grave by the Marne,
the visitor from the country didn't have the gift of clairvoyance,
didn't see the new class of gentlemen in the historical window,
just plebs everywhere you looked

the Military Academy was for the sons of entitled persons, no, he
was not entitled, not at all, not descended from anyone who left
their lives on the battlefield, in his case it was more someone who
had climbed up into the air, vanished into the clouds, dissolved
into the lofty blue ether, no, not a bed-wetter, but the general,
maybe Bismarck, was dead, he was partaking now of the peace of
God, not on the battlefield, medals and honors, consolations of
religion, seven gun salutes from a guard of honor, the child was
helpless, he detested them, the back end of a bronze horse

free education till confirmation or the completion of his fifteenth
year, they told his mother, rancid moldy bacon from the mouse-
trap, not a penny to pay, he's a millstone round your neck, and
she began to believe he prevented her from going to sew on the
estates, from patching the sheets, sometimes sitting with her at
table, sometimes not, and he sat alone in her room, neglected, as
they say, and he ate up her bread-token bread, she got a mark per
sewing day, with free board thrown in (though in the kitchen)

the Commander runs the whole organization and is its public
face to the outside world, Colonel von Froser, he clopped on
horseback from the fort into the town, weathered local celebrity in constant representation of His Majesty, white helmet feathers, white moustache, sharp snappy spurs, the whole man snappy

and sharp, chamois leather spreading behind, taking parade on
foot jerky as in the first regiment of Grenadier Guards, his boss
His Majesty the Emperor of all the Russias, Nicholas the second
of that ilk, unfortunately a foe, and a former cousin and no longer an Imperial Majesty

he exercises the disciplinary power of a regimental commander
over the officers and the rest of the military personnel, fought battles in sandboxes, came out of the bush like Zieten, didn't hang
around at Sedan, went straight on to take Paris, senior commander on the bend of the Seine, not unforgiving in his dreams, didn't
string anyone up, modest in triumph, dined at Maxim's with the
Marquis de Belfort-Saint Lehar, cork-popping jollity, louloufrou-
froudoudou, picture postcards to Frau von Froser of the great
scenes, the Tuileries, the Invalides under German colors, and of
course the Hall of Mirrors at Versailles blackwhitered from now
to all eternity

the officers each have two companies of boys under their command, commanded them to the barrage, there was one Moloch
called Western Front, there were other Molochs no less hungry,
their names were Eastern Front Isonzo Front and Dardanelles
Front and there was the Sea Front too which was acquainted with
the Leviathan and the Sun flung Icarus down from the sky

minor derelictions are punished by a simple rebuke a rebuke before the assembled unit or cleaning-details performance of punishment duties out of turn report three times and the allocation of
punishment, that was the business of the scaly souls, the pinched
greasers that remained at the bottom even if they were on top,
the dry-seed sadistic love-good-order-it-will-love-you-back men
who secured the protection of submissive servants and kept accounts in their glory, up to and including the honorable account
of death, always *comme il faut*, drunk on orders, the hand not
trembling, but moved by the great epoch and in silent joy

their remit comprises the physical training of the boys the teaching of swimming and gymnastic exercises as well as the supervision of attire physical cleanliness dormitories wash- and cleaning-rooms, they were posts for inverts, a real treasure trove, no pinkypink bar, the classic Sparta of the pedophile pedagogue, the honorable altar of the old welted goddess Artemis, sheet lifters, let's see what you've got and is it clean, a phalanx of young backs, bend over, more more, two smooth firm pillars of muscle a straight cleft clean as a whistle tormenting shudders down one's spine, the military swimming baths white ten meter board in the sleet algal green water goose pimples, the damp mouthed military swimming trunks a red triangle red pudendal rag red blur in your eyes, the shrill whistle of the man in charge

the academy chaplain—Lutheran—is responsible for the souls of all members of the academy, the teachers are placed under him, he conducts lessons gives confirmation classes and supervises the classrooms and the teaching materials, a man of the letter, toughly resisting ill report, old gent of the Corps Pomerania, patriotic soldier of God, housemaster *in excelsis*, Christian Jehovah, turning down his cuirassier's boots, translating Luther's Bible into Prussian, loved injunctions, obey authority give unto Caesar what is Caesar's and spare the whip spoil the child

I looked down onto the barracks yard, gazed upon the barracks yard, I found it empty, a bare rectangle, a barren space among the brick buildings of the dormitories, worn down by standing at attention and goose-stepping. The yard lay there terrorized. The soldiers had quit it, wind and rain made free with it. For days on end now. The yard was clean. It shone as though freshly washed. I savored the unusual silence, chewed it like cotton wool, cushiony bloating constipating wool-soft tangles, dosed with anesthetic, soaked in stimulant. Bells should have pealed, a Te Deum sounded, a new life begun; but even the sirens were silent. I had never seen the exercise yard so peaceful, no yells, no violence, no fear, no humiliated individuals issuing orders or receiving orders, at most at night, in moonlight, but at night I would never have dared to go up to the window, I wouldn't have been allowed to

look out at the yard, I had to sleep even if I wasn't asleep but
shuddering instead, and even then the yard wouldn't have been
empty, the sentries would have been pacing up and down, how
tensely I would have listened to their mechanical footfall, I knew
they were wearing ankle-length gray coats with the collars turned
up, puffed up squires, faceless puppets in an evil puppet theater,
their fixed bayonets aglint in the starlight, their elongated shadows lapping at the yard, shadows of wolves, wolf muzzles, wolf
teeth, wolf claws, and oh, they watched over my sleep, my suffering, my rage, my incarceration, wolf breath enwrapped me.
Armed, spraddle-legged giants had stood on the now betrayed,
bleached, infertile bloody sand. The giants had fought against me.
The horrible giants had entered the lists against me. The giants
had gnawed at me, day after day. For a whole year the monstrous
man-eating giants had fought against me, but God had taken pity
on me, he had led them away, and I wished them a hero's grave.

I stood by the window in the hospital wing. I was in a dream, but
I no longer trusted dreams. At any moment, I might fall back into
miserable reality, the yapping of the hellhounds could leap at me,
sold and enslaved they might be, but relishing the opportunities
afforded them of service, who had offered themselves, who had
bent over, who had distinguished themselves by their ordinariness, slipped into the battle tunic or the gray work overall with
cotton ties, a black and white tie for company commander, a yellow one for dormitory-prefect, and a shoulder button for squad-
leader, my comrades, they tore us out of sleep, chucked us out of
bed, they had no need to chase me, all night I was trembling in ex-
pectation of their call, I had seen day break already, creeping cold-
ly over the rows of beds, dawn for early death, a popular song, and
march into the washroom, march into the latrine, a driven herd,
at the end of it as for all herds was the slaughterhouse, an old rat-
tling roller, reports that said nothing, they were delivered and
taken cognizance of, coffee was not drunk, a scorched smelling
black liquid was taken, potato bread and beet jam were wolfed
down, fermenting in the flat boyish bellies, out into the yard, fall
in, counted off, to be sure no one had gone missing, marched out

in units, the roll-call, the Imperial war flag on the pole, the Major in his Home Front get up, his lieutenants in field gray, Verdun had not been taken, the junior officers wore colored peace-tunics, what were they doing here, the teachers came along in ideological weskits, the academy chaplain like a sick moon, the supply of scarecrows was unaffected even after four years of war, exercises began, push-ups, star-jumps, knee bends, report, salute, saluting was a particular obsession with them, it was deep inside them, it was the intransigence and glory of the proud Reich, even Verdun and the conquest of Verdun seemed to depend on the fact that no one who was in possession of a piece of string, a button, or an epaulette, might be disregarded. The hospital tunic of blue and white striped fustian dropped onto my feet like a sack. I was trapped in the sack like a lunatic in his straitjacket. I was twelve years old. They had shaved my head. I could see myself in the misted window of the hospital wing looking like an ancient shaven-headed convict. I was the junior in the fourth company of the military academy. I was Germany's future. The iron beds reared out behind me from the whitewashed wall like so many tumid penises. The beds were Government Issue beds, they were built to order, they were rough, flat, hard-edged, hard. Only the bed on which I had lain was messy and drew attention to itself. The hard excelsior pillow, the rough, patched horse-blanket both smelled of fever. The floor stank of licorice and gun-grease. It had all been a castle once upon a time. Drafts from bygone wars pushed through cracks and rubble. The knights had slaughtered the knights. In the cannon stoves there were no fires. The long stovepipes made their way icily and idly up to the lofty ceiling. I was all alone. They all had run away, left, been collected, the barking hell-hounds, the little useful devils, the smashing giants, they had seen the writing on the wall, they had hightailed it. I had won. On the whitewashed wall hung the picture of the Kaiser, hung Hindenburg and Ludendorff. The Kaiser and his chiefs of staff leaned down photogenically over the general staff map. They had great plans for me. The glowing red trim on their uniforms had heated the fever of my flu. A hero's death was a glowing Moloch with three helmeted heads. Aspirin, the stern staff doctor had shouted, and that same night had died of my flu. God had protected me even against the staff doctor. The red flag blew over the barracks gate. Poor, heavy thing, it flapped foggily in the chill wind. Of course it also rang out bright and promising against the gray November day. The sign meant nothing to me, but it signified that there was such a thing as a miracle, that I was free, that I had overcome the hero's death and the flu death, that I was allowed home, and had won the war.

She opened the door and closed it behind her, she was in the ward, the abandoned, the reprieved hospital that was nothing but a smell, decomposed, on the Nessus shirt of the empty beds the leftovers of sweat, stains of the crucified who had lain there, masturbated or refrained, died or run off, my mother was come to get me, she hesitated, she was afraid, she was late, she was the last, she was come out of the old collapsing Reich, she was the end of German history, she didn't draw a deep breath, she didn't gaze out into the dawn, she stopped by the door, she didn't take another step. Perhaps the trains weren't running, the locomotives had no coal, or the royal timetable had been adapted to serve the revolution and the retreat, the carriages had hastened to Berlin, to the escaped Kaiser, the orphaned palace, sailors from Kiel, gunners from the battle cruisers, with flags, with rifles, decked out with flowers, withered roses from August, it was November, or my mother had had to borrow the money for the dangerous journey; and who would have lent it to her? The simple soldierly green on the door my mother was standing in front of had splintered with war and the passage of time, there were white cracks spreading in the green like the delta of a mighty river from my geography book, the Ganges with ash-heaps on its banks, snakes and wealthy vultures, enviable fakirs, or the reedy courses of the Nile, on which Moses had drifted in his basket when he was banished to serve God, but it could also be the Mississippi and a sack full of Indians, pirates and crocodiles, my mother was standing in front of this map, before a surveyor's table on which strategic positions were to be drawn, where victories could not be designed, she didn't trust herself, she stopped where she was, looked at me or down at her feet, at the boards trampled with hobnailed boots. She was shy. I'm no longer sure if I saw it or imagined it. My mother was young, but the green and white riverine landscape of the door darkened her. My mother was abashed, and it was me abashing her, I always had done, the sight of me awoke fear and remorse in her, I shocked and tormented her, I could feel it, she had no need to shout it out, she stopped in front of the line of beds, looked at the beds in their deranged order, I was pained by our weakness, hers and mine, how could she love me, I could hardly even stand up, or stay on my feet, and now I wanted to run over to her and got tangled up in my long blue and white striped Prussian nightshirt. The planks swayed. A ship was going down. Huge thunder. The lifeboats were set adrift, the waves pushed them down. The painting of the Kaiser fell off the wall. The frame broke, glass splintered, the fragments cut into my feet. Hindenburg and Ludendorff were fighting or mating together like dogs, they were dancing in each other's jaws and they opened the ball. The educational battalion was celebrating His Majesty's birthday. The party had been moved forward, all the later dates were already spoken for, the dance cards had been given away, it was the last hurrah. I fell, or I saw myself falling, I stumbled against my mother, I pressed my burning face against her young body, hugged it close, it was flat and chaste, not warm and squirming with birth like a family bed, not like the wife of the Major, all the boys had mothers I didn't like. I sobbed, but I got control of myself, I had learned to do that, I had attended an educational establishment, I was a recruit in a brave land, I was the steadfast tin soldier in the fairy story, I got a grip on myself, as I had been ordered to, I stood upright, the stern orders, the cornet signals of dressage burst in the stormy air, I looked straight at my mother, I didn't look away, I didn't rush towards her, I didn't fall down, I didn't clutch at her, I didn't cry, I didn't save her the way through the ward, I let her slowly run the gauntlet of the empty beds, I saw her smaller than life coming towards me, it seemed to me she was observing me through a reversed telescope, through a long lens that makes its object disappear instead of bringing it closer, and I was smaller too, suddenly I was a narrow-minded military observer, poisoned, made sadistic by the sadism of the system: I blamed my mother for us both standing there, so poor, so deprived in the silent ward, the barracks, the square, the garrison, the bleak town. I felt like screaming and lashing out at her. But we stopped still and mute. Only later did I attack my mother, in order to rob her. It was retaliation; only I never knew against whom.

A train left that night. Our breath froze on the window. A candle burned, a guttering stub, they called it a Hindenburg light. We sat pressed together, sniffing the sodden wool of our old overcoats, barely able to see each other. One man said Karl Liebknecht had proclaimed the republic. Another man protested vehemently, no, it was Scheidemann. Everyone squabbled in the cold compartment. They held newspapers up against the flickering candle. The newspapers were called things like "Freedom" or "The Red Flag" and they were the short-lived revolutionary supplements of local gazettes. In grainy pictures I made out a man in a wide-brimmed hat, but one of the other men in the compartment pointed to a different picture with a man who was waving a round or bowler hat. The background was supposed to be the Reichstag or the Imperial Palace, which my teachers had described for me in such glowing terms. In the end, no one cared. But the names stuck: Liebknecht and Scheidemann. My mother slept with her head in my lap. The train slowly crossed the bridge over the Oder. The iron struts of the bridge creaked, and I thought we would fall into the dark water, and never live to experience what was coming next, my time. Morning paled. At the end of the bridge, sentries stretched holding their rifles muzzles down. This seemed to be my victory, the wreck of discipline. The soldiers wore white armbands with something written on them, but they were too far away and I couldn't read them.

Childish fear night fever dimmed lights, then the pattern of the wallpaper slipped down next to my bed, the wall crumbled, material was dissolving, I clearly registered it, and saw the truth, the illusory picture of the world disappeared, I was fourteen, and three or four degrees above the red line on the thermometer were sufficient to conjure the revelations of sacred drugs, the Mexican horror of the glass coffin, body and soul turned to stone with full consciousness.

I had won the war, but it was hard to celebrate the victory on my own, with everyone else claiming to have lost something: they didn't rightly know what. Of course I saw them, the unhappy ones who had lost a leg or an arm or another joint, or their face, the gas-victims with yellow-green skin, spluttering the minor remnants of their lives out of corroded lungs, those who had been buried alive and were still shaking, and the women had sons and husbands and the children had fathers they never saw again, and some had lost property, or were in the process of losing it now, piece by piece, the inherited home, the brooch for the black formal dress, the widow's ring, coins had already been melted down in exchange for iron, they had a piece of paper pinned up on a wall or tucked away in the cupboard, the Kaiser thanked them for their generous donation, the Crown Prince thanked them in his black hussar's uniform, his cap set at a jaunty angle, the death's head cheeky, the iron Hindenburg added his thanks, some Chancellor, no, not Bismarck, not the Iron Chancellor, a different one, the signature was illegible and no one could think of the name, it was in a better way with the painted history of a Fräulein von Schmettau, the lofty picture had been received in return for the gold, a young lady who had cut off her blond hair a hundred years ago, and a century of emotion sacrificed on the altar of the fatherland, that was Prussia, so said all the old elementary schoolteachers, and the secondary schoolteachers, and the Professors at the University said so as well, and they wore their watches on chains of iron, on a ribbon of little Iron Crosses, instead of on the simple or lavish chain left them by grandfather or from their confirmation, brought to God and His word, said the mothers looking proudly at their sons in their blue suits, their long blue trousers, the blue outsize men's hats, their stiff white hands in their stiff white gloves, and the grown up sons of the upright old gentlemen wore Iron Crosses over their bellies which were still round or pointy, with what, oh, with rutabaga or with bran-bread or the secretly slaughtered pig, not to mention those who beside themselves and screaming insisted they had lost their honor, and if you talked about the passage of history, cut the grimmest faces, whereas otherwise they behaved like everybody else, laughed at silly jokes and damage done to others, or were perfectly serious, sad, concerned, hungry, in love, lustful and furious, because life went on, in the end they all said that, a trite phrase for sure, spoken over graves, over the many little crosses of iron or wood and also on newspapers stretching as far as the horizon and beyond, but no one I met appeared to have understood that he himself had lost everything, arm leg face father husband son brother goods and chattels even honor on the day that war was declared, and that four years later there was only something to be won, which was peace: but they didn't rate peace.

I was a witness, but I wasn't there in person, it's possible I was lying in bed when it happened, it's quite likely, I went to bed early, though often also I went to bed late, sometimes I hadn't even got up in the morning or at lunchtime, and I didn't need to go to bed in the evening, but I wasn't asleep in bed, or I wasn't always asleep, or I slept little, even when I was in bed, I would talk to Macbeth in bed, a German forest was a German forest, it wasn't Macbeth's forest, it wasn't Birnam Wood, and Macbeth had no need to fear the forest: no German forest ever marched to Dunsinane. I wandered with Hyperion over the heights of Arcady. I read poems by a man by the name of Benn, or another by the name of Becher. I took ship with river pirates on the warm mud-soupy Mississippi, and under the skin of the river drifting like rotten tree trunks phosphoresced the old Leviathans of the Good Book. Plato also visited me in my bed: even Echecrates, because I had admired Socrates before, but never so much as now. Green wallpaper! Whoever stuck it down was either dead or in hospital. Mold was green: that was my fortress sure, my camp, my mattressphere. Kitty-cornered was my mother's bed, it was empty on that evening or at that hour, later on my mother's bed was always occupied, and later still it was always empty, until finally I sold it or it was lost. Then there was the table where we sat when my mother was home and there was something to eat, or where we sat when there was nothing to eat and we just sat, and sometimes we talked to each other and sometimes we didn't, and we got along or we didn't. In the cupboard was the bread when we had bread, and my mother kept the cupboard locked when she went out to work, so that I wouldn't eat up the bread, but I had a nail that I'd bent and managed to flatten, and with that nail I was able to pick the useless lock of the old cupboard, and I took the bread and bit off a piece, and I stuffed myself on the bread, and it choked me because I knew it would make my mother cry. An electric bulb hung from braided wires under the low ceiling, it burned feebly and wasn't supposed to burn at all, I was supposed to be either asleep or sitting in the dark, if I switched the light on I was wasting it, my mother wasn't able to cut it off, but then a man came with a bill and he cut it off, and then we both sat in the dark, my mother and me, and a woman who had come to us had called the bulb naked, a naked bulb, and I liked that, a naked bulb, naked light, they put up a tent, outside was the town, the enemy, the enemy in the field, there were wolves and hunters in the forest, and on the ripped wool blanket I wrapped myself in were books from all the libraries of the town and the university, and Pastor Koch, seeing the books said, you're not a Bolshevist are you, and I looked at him, and I counted the dueling scars in his feisty red face, and I asked him what's a Bolshevist, and I looked through him perhaps as far as Russia, and then there were the magazines our town was avid for, and that I delivered for Alt's bookstore, and they had names like "The Bachelor," "Colour Magazine" and "New Life." They could have taught me what life is. I never learned. I didn't know what girls looked like, and whether they looked the way they looked in the pages of the new magazines wearing little or nothing and like boys who went skinny-dipping and got aroused, and the girls were as sleek as the backs of the boys, and if I had previously avoided the other boys in the schoolyard, now I wanted a boy I could wrestle with, wrestle with naked and not for sport, and I looked for one and couldn't find him, and some of the girls were plump and round, and I neither loved them nor hated them, I stripped off my shirt, it was the only shirt I had, I

wore it at night and I wore it by day, and we had a kitchen as well,
the kitchen was next to the bedroom, and I trotted across the bedroom and trotted barefoot across the brick floor of the kitchen,
and I felt the brick under my naked feet, cold and worn and
somehow soft, the cold bricks felt soothing to my feet, they were
like the girls, smooth, gentle, plump and cold, I heard as I trotted
about on the kitchen bricks how the mice scuttled over the crumbling cement unlit stove, and hid in the kindling I collected in the
forest, or didn't hide at all, just sat in the unlit stove, because I had
failed to gather any wood, and I thought while I trotted about in
the kitchen, why are they afraid of me, I want to talk to the mice,
and why do they stay here, there's nothing here for them, and I
opened the door out of the kitchen straight into the yard, and I
listened in the yard and listened to the night, the night was silent,
the town was silent, a silent town, a silent globe, we lived in the
yard, we lived in a barn, in the front house a solitary harmless
light burned in the window of the old slipper-maker, even at
night he pulled the thread through the tough felt, he was a cot-
tage industry and an old man, and whatever work he did in the
day or at night was poorly recompensed, and he kept the Bible
open beside him while he worked, because he was old and he was
afraid of death, but I could hear the hosannas of angels, it was
January, the air was frozen like brittle glass about to burst, I trotted about naked in the crisp snow, on the splintering ice sheeting
the puddles, I hung naked on the bent carpet rail over the door, I
did pull-ups, one, two, three, I exhausted myself doing dozens of
pull-ups, from the yard next door I could hear the butcher's dog
whimpering because he was afraid just as the slipper-maker was
afraid, and the dog whimpered softly because he feared his master
even more than he feared death, this was Master Hergesell, who
had come back from Verdun missing his right leg and something
else too, people whispered, and now demanded his right leg and
whatever else back from his wife or back from his dog, both of
whom he beat, and from all the animals whom he slaughtered,
and I felt a ray from heaven, a starburst went through me, and
struck the frozen snowy ground: on the heights, on the beetling
cliff, where I liked to feel my tears my boyish cheeks already felt

your magic breath. Or not in bed and not in the yard. I walked an old woman through the town, she hung feeble and heavy on my arm, midnight had struck, three towers were watching over us, St Nikolai, St. Jakob, and St. Maria, their clocks had struck the last chime of twelve, and pushed the day over the line, into non-existence to where we were just able still to discern it, though now impalpable to our senses and cheerless the wasted hour, the day unlived, the examination failed, lapsed into the dark, irretrievable and forever lost. The streets were deserted, the squares were deserted, the houses were pretty coffins all in a row. Footfall resounded, echo bounced back, the fishwives were asleep with their fish, the fish market was a fish-mouth, mute. The town council lacked counsel, its lofty gables were crumbling. God was working his purpose out, if you happened to believe. Shadows, if there was a moon, light-flowers by flickering gaslight. I did it for money. The old lady was paying me a million, or paying me a billion, she shelled out an astronomical wage on me, and the sloppily printed, newly pressed, and already somehow tatty notes assured honorable gentlemen that somewhere, sometime or even at any hour of their choosing, at some counter or other they would be paid a million or a billion or a quintillion in gold for the piece of paper, I can't remember, I could never find the counter, or I found it but at the wrong time, but the honorable gentlemen were not perturbed, and they threatened you with prison if you were foolish enough to copy or forge their splendid notes. I should have thrown the money in the gutter. The old woman was quaking, and she was clinging to the hope that I could protect her from the spirits of the night. But spirits are able to open even locked wards of asylums, and who was I to try and bolt them again? Did I even want to? The old woman was mistaken in me, but perhaps she just thought if I walk with him I won't be out alone at night. But I knew that they did, or had already done so, and I thought Macbeth, Hyperion, the river pirates, Gottfried Benn's little aster, Becher's oriflamme on the lips, the old woman on my arm, slowly, step by step, I had been killed, and it was certain that they meant me, but I could equally well have been the culprit, the fellow with the shovel in his hand. You are the murderer, you are the designated victim, I raise my hand, I strike, or I suffer it to happen, I hide, I am Cain, but I am also Abel, and you are Cain and Abel. And where is God, looking on and suffering it to happen, and all because of some ridiculous smoke? We are always witnesses, unreliable, cowardly witnesses who haven't seen anything, who don't know anything, you are my contemporary, there are generals who manage everything, we put them into service once God disappointed us, or we set our faces against Him, we sewed the red collars for the generals, we dyed their collars with our blood, generals are as plentiful as sand by the sea, and the art of commanding men is the most widespread of all the gifts, and it offers a solid and desirable career, when it comes down to it the general will win the battle and lose the war, he will become president of a chastened nation, and in the end he will triumph over everyone in his memoirs, he will become a memorial, he will be cast in bronze, oh, generals are good with numbers, they may miscalculate in the big odds, but never in the little things that are necessary to get a war going. The generals count up what is growing, they bundle it up by years, and when they have enough years, their speculation on death comes off. I was indignant when I learned of it. The general called up all those born in one year. What gave him the right? What was he thinking of? The general is dead, no, the general is immortal, he draws his pension, in the morning you see him walk in the park, an upright, unbowed figure. I am alive, I suspect you, you are my year, I will call you up. How repulsive you are to me when you strip naked, and stand before the draft commission, stick out your bottom for them to beat you. Are you so patient at other times? I want to tell our story, my story, your story, it's nothing to do with you, I am just telling it to myself, I will expose you, you are not yet sufficiently naked. It's disagreeable to be the witness, annoying to be the culprit, stupid to be the body, after so many years. You can't remember, you've lost your memory, a conscience you never had, you know nothing. The best thing is being the prosecutor. His anger is always righteous. You might not believe him, but that doesn't matter. The court needs him. To a lot of people he's a familiar figure. They saw him under the trees with a shovel. He is the worst. He handed me the shovel, he called out: Hit him. Now he is accusing you. He is serious. He is a serious man. I joke, and I'm no match for him. He calls for my head. He is always calling for someone's head, that's how it is with his seriousness. I will have you called to the witness stand. Your evidence will not save us. We are condemned from the outset.

I thought at the time that I was waking up, but probably the truth is that my sleep passed into a dream. I saw myself acting in this dream, I acted reasonably, following some dream logic; but I couldn't have said at any stage what I was dreaming about, or where I was headed. Nor is it possible to say that I was drifting. Sometimes I may have made a claim of the sort (to whom? Who was I talking to?), but it wasn't true. I hadn't decided on anything, not even on drifting; only I aimed insistently away from the others, and that was what mattered to me.

The room is large and cold, it's cold in a warm sort of way, it's dark, the black furniture makes the room dark, the heavy black furniture doesn't make the room small, it makes it into a sort of mountain range, the heavy black furniture creates fronts, the cupboard threatens the table, the table rears up against the chair, the heavy black furniture resembles so many fortresses of solid, black-reflecting wood, large black knights and little black prisoners are shadow-jousting, the black desk is up on black lion's feet, the carved black lion's feet claw the black carpet, the wool of the black lamb lies shredded under the black feet, the black portiere seals off the black universe, the dismal drawling dirge-like drone of the classes remains outside, the drone of the alphabet, the drone of the multiplication tables, the drone of the still baffling mathematical formula, the drone of the already holey law of nature, the drone of the carefully put-together sentence that says nothing, the drone of the hymn heard by no god, the drone of the patriotic song that intoxicates its singer, the drone of the battles of Frederick the Great, the drone of the battles of Bismarck, the drone of the chanted battles of the Kaiser, the non-drone of the silence following the question what do we do now, the drone of hatred against the present, the Republic, Weimar, Versailles, the black and red and German humiliation; remains the interrupted but still flowing stream making for the dangerous rapids, the waterfall where time stops or ends or has never been or begins again or is like today, remains the great Poor that the boy takes home on his report card, outside remain the smells with which the boy is familiar, that he flees from, that he can never escape, the smell of the thick lard and onion sandwich, the black pudding between floury clots of salt, that disagrees with him and that he doesn't want, that he drops in the dirt when high-handedness insists on giving it to him anyway, remains the acrid sweat of fear at school, the sour keenness of the swots, the proud scabbed knees of the bad boys, that they bare in winter to the frost.

I'm standing in front of the headmaster, I am a body, I have a soul too but I am losing my soul, I have to be careful I don't lose it altogether, but my body has a soul as well, and with my body's soul which crowds my other, true soul, I can feel my body and I stand in my body in the world. I don't wear underclothes, even though my mother wants me to, although my undershirt and pants are torn, I am just wearing my striped sailor's shirt, wearing it on bare skin, and a pair of blue shorts, I grew out of both those things, it's summer, but I wish I could go around like that in the depths of winter too, with bare legs, bare thighs, to feel the frost on my skin, and to feel my body in the frost, as it rubs itself against the too-tight seams of shirt and shorts, and the constriction tells me I have something, namely me, and that understanding gives me power, even over the headmaster. The headmaster is a heavily built man. His hair is brush-cut like Hindenburg's. High top boots would suit him, and a breastplate and an eagle helmet. He sits heavily behind his heavy desk, and looks at me dispassionately out of his tiny murky eyes. The air is full of cold cigar smoke. That's the smell of power. Coal-merchant Kleuke has that smell as well. Susemihl has it. Our bills are unpaid. We are unable to open any more accounts. The headmaster asks me my name.

I am annoyed, he must know my name, I go to his school, I try not to go to his school, his school torments me, I hate it, I hate him, and he doesn't know my name. Do I have a name? Have I forgotten it? Will I have to look for a new one? I find it difficult, it makes me break out in sweat to have to tell the headmaster my name. The headmaster makes a grunt like some animal that rootles around in the earth with its trunk. Who knows what he's snuffling after. Thinking of him as an animal makes him easier to bear. I don't hate the headmaster nearly as much as I hate Herr Krüger, who is my form teacher. Herr Krüger never looked at me with indifference. He never forgot my name. In his eyes I see the gleam of the huntsman tracking his quarry. I have spent three years trying to escape from Herr Krüger, and I hope I have got away. Often Herr Krüger would seem to have caught up with me, to be about to catch me, and throw me to the ground, but I always managed to get away and escape into terrain where he couldn't follow me. Come on out of there, tell me what you're thinking, he demanded, his lips were pressed together, the brownish muscles twitched in his bony cheeks, and I looked straight at him, pale with hatred, but unafraid, and I said nothing. Herr Krüger did not manage to drive me into his herd, he didn't stamp me with the brand of usefulness, he didn't recruit me for the Bismarck Society or the Submariners Society, he didn't manage to convert me to any of his principles.

The headmaster pulls a bundle of papers, a file out of a drawer in his desk, he opens the file, he looks at me, unsmiling as he sees me standing in front of him, he says quietly that the decision is not mine, but that my mother would have to take me out of school.

I thought I had to threaten my mother and simultaneously bribe her to take me out of school, and my threat was that I would stay in bed and never get up again, while my bribe was that, once free of school, I would earn money to help her. But it wasn't necessary to threaten or bribe my mother, because she was less aware of the gravity of the step than I was, and, perhaps enfeebled by the struggle of her daily life, she was prepared to let me be something that could look after itself, and no more; she was inclined

albeit against her occasional dreams about my future, particularly early on, to let me be something, let me slip into a class whose
members she had disdained when a girl, and even now as a woman. She couldn't understand that I had no sense of social position,
that I didn't look up to some people or look down on others, but
saw in all forms of existence merely varieties of disguise that didn't
particularly suit me. In the end, though, when we talked about
it, we both believed my claim that I would earn money. And so
I thought I could step into the welter of life and take off the un-
comfortably small and outgrown cloak of my childhood.

He walked around the Town Hall, the beautiful stately barn of a
building, the Schildbürger town hall, his town hall stood firm in
the rain, in the fog, in the snow, in the harsh jangling frost, in the
white nights of the Baltic summers, and as ever not knowing what
to do, he walked across the fish market, the fishwives were sleeping with the dead fish, he crossed the Main Market, the geese,
the wise birds of Juno, had come over from the island of Rügen
in boats, in the market their throats were slashed open, and their
blood stained the cobbles, mingling with the blood of pirates who
had been beheaded there once in the distant past, and the blood
of the poor who had been shot there in the more recent past, the
turnip women had slumped down on the feathers of the slaughtered geese with Gaia, the ancient fertility goddess, and both were
calmly sleeping the sleep of the just

what happened on the day of mobilization? The lieutenant and
his men marched out into the market, the soldiers knocked over
the stalls of the market women, the mayor stepped out of the
town hall, the apothecary came out of his apothecary's shop, the
post office workers left the post office, in their blue uniforms they
resembled soldiers, they looked like sturdy fathers in the sturdy
infantry, the fish women turned as mute as their fish, the berry
women wept, the old houses on the market place scented blood,
experienced historic gables, reliable witnesses to sundry fatali-
ties, Herr Störtebecker, reverend Herr von Wallenstein Excellency, our dear Protestant Majesty Gustavus Adolphus and Luther's

not Münzer's fortress sure, things were lively in Rutenberg's wine parlor, numerous Frenchmen had their necks broken, claret was knocked back, there was thunderous popping and fizzing, the District President came along in riding boots Count Baer-Baerenhof, the police captain stood at attention, Wangerin's school bookshop put out more flags, the blackwhitered colors, the colors black and white and slightly sheepish, the red falcon on white ground, the Lieutenant grasped fate in his white gloves, Long Live the Kaiser, they yelled it out three times, the sky inspected them with piercing eye, the soldiers looked bravely at the bright sun, two weeks later the lieutenant and his men were all dead

he wandered along the Lange Strasse, he was on his way to work, on his way to the dive called the Bat, he walked slowly, the town was quiet, it was after midnight, it was still too early, the moon would shine when it shone, the light of heaven brushed the rooftops, nature was dead, he had been standing in front of shop windows, in front of Erdmann's department store, in front of Sparagani's sweetshop, and then for a long time in front of the windows of the three university bookshops, and all the windows were dark, the street-lights were turned off, only around the old gaslights was there a pale glimmer, a nimbus that didn't properly develop, but in the dark and who knows empty Christmas windows of the shops he had seen what he had wanted to see, what might perhaps once have been there and no longer was, except in his memory, in Erdmann's it was the dazzling chrome pedal car and the Noah's Ark with animals all in wood, the puppet theater with the figures of the clown, the Jew, the crocodile, and death, the lead Indians and some Friedrich Wilhelm or other's bodyguard with tall caps as if twisted out of old newspapers, the Kaiser's field howitzers, the dying warriors clutching the flag firmly in their grip, the little town with its red roofs, the town hall and the church, so peaceful and phony, the train trundling round it, incessantly, all Advent long, and at Sparagani's the big chocolate cake, and the other fat cake with the model of the university picked out in cream and marzipan in a ring of crystallized orange slices, but the displays of the university bookshop didn't need to be raised by mem-

ory out of the night, or maybe they did, precious things, Grimm's
Märchen in a tattered Reklam paper edition and Aladdin's lamp
and wonderful journeys in the orient, the far isles, the secrets of
the Chinese, fortunate survivals of shipwrecks, also the book of
the Iron Chancellor and the navy calendar, the colonial calendar,
and the good companion for good boys and the New Universe for
well-brought-up boys who wanted to rule the universe, who were
drilled to conquer the world, conquer the water, conquer the air,
perhaps conquer the moon, no more white empty stains on maps
of the earth or the heavens, no terra incognita, no distant hope,
no utopia anywhere, but he didn't want to see those things he already had and had read, and he wanted as little to see what he
would have seen by light, the memoirs of Ludendorff, of the Kaiser, of the Crown Prince, the justifications of their generals and
the white book about the humiliation of Versailles and the black
book about the black disgrace on the Rhine, he was on the look-
out for other things that weren't to be found here, the invective
against the times, the books of a new society, the signs of change.

Behind the shop door hung a newspaper, and he read in
the glimmer of the gaslight that Lenin had died. Thereupon he
wished he had a black tie to slip on, or to tie in a knot, the way
artists had once done, like Wagner, who was also present in the
bookshop. He slowly approached the Bat, saw the red light of her
name above the blacked out windows, heard the piano-playing of
the ancient Frau Kasch, whom he was supposed to collect and escort home after closing time. It was always dark in the Bat, wom-
en sat on the tables, or under the tables, and the men at the tables
were strangely excited by the women on or under the tables. They
laughed or grunted or yelled and had red faces from the subdued
light of the red lamps. He walked past them without seeing them.
Frau Kasch patiently played operetta tunes, and, later on, when
everyone was past noticing and she was exhausted, she played the
Marche Funebre of Chopin. She was blind, and when he looked
at her, he saw the blind Homer; her face was an antique face. Her
daughter was locked up in the insane asylum, committed to the
care of others that was no care, on the other side of the tracks.
Night and day in her bed she could hear the trains going between

Sweden and Berlin, and she could have escaped the town if she'd gone on time. Käte Kasch had been a friend of his mother's when they were both young.

The university was built in commemoration of what triumph? The world famous founder donor builder—help me out. Where? How? Who? Not a dog in Teheran, not a lion in the forest, not even the humiliated captive behind bars in the smutty menagerie of our fair, no black man, no yellow brother, not even who knows who in the new world knows his name, not to mention the white patches, the brightly dressed or naked men, the monsters of sea or land or sky in the projections of Mercator or Visser. No point in wasting time looking. Who knows him here, the world-famous wise man? Not kings, knights, peasants, beggars, maybe the tailor who makes his bespoke suits, the cobbler who makes his hand-made shoes, the baker of his daily bread. A slick eulogy, current small change in the republic of knowledge. Disreputable association. Of course they could be proud of their fine martyr's board: the ones they brained, stoned, burned, exterminated with fire and sword, locked in dungeons, offered the cup of poison, drove into exile. For nothing, for phantasms, illusions, progress, freedom, understanding, truth or what they took to be truth. But he is not conceited, he doesn't mind not knowing. Whosoever's bread I eat, his song I sing, a subject of any authority, heaven as instructed by any passing pontifex, his most submissive subject. The world-famous author, then, of a devotional history. What can he mean? What delights him so, what does he edify with? In the beginning was desert and darkness, and it was light, and Adam met Eve, and Cain envied Abel. A thousand years, millions of years. Loads of lovely victories, the earth lay there like a flat plate, circling in the amniotic fluid of majesty, now it was a ball, a star among myriad stars displaced from the center of creation; until further notice. But he insists, here and now, and he insists also, there and now, hard to believe, the antipode. Two philosophers in slippers or in top-boots, also in patent leather pumps, sole to sole, and between them the flying orb. Amazing equilibrists. There was Moses and the great Aristotle, the even greater Alexander and Nero and Virgil and Charlemagne, Peter and his representatives, and maybe Mohammed of the holy Kaba as far as the gates of Vienna, there was strange news of one Buddha, Jesuit gossip, and some Hutzli- putzli took ship with madmen and gold. There remained the busy researcher of the history of our dear native land. The important personage throws himself in the dirt, scrabbles and crows like a cock on a dung heap, and finds his atlas of Pomeranian pre-histo- ry. A Professor with a Chair. A truly Secret Councillor. Who was foolish enough to ask him for true and secret advice? The sitter on the Chair. There he stands, grips fast, and could do otherwise. En- titled to vote in the royal learned societies at Copenhagen or Up- psala. Welcome halo of the magician from the north, dazzled by polar light, he shut his eyes, wouldn't join in, but chimed in, had no money to travel. Corresponding member, several letters in ar- rears, or else he never got replies, the Royal Academy in London, the Institut de France in Paris. London, never discovered, never saw it, perhaps listened to Kant on London. Colleague hadn't been there either. Paris, city of the blessed kings, throne of the great kings, of St. Bartholomew's and certain other nights. The residence of the sun, *quartier* of the *grandes écoles*, fire of rebellion, the chamber of Pascal, dream over. Dean of the Faculty. Fruit of years. Now himself magnificence. It was time. His lectern set up too high for him. Death peers over his shoulder. A weight on his back, pressure against his neck. Or was it life, his proud career, miserable stipends, wintry seminaries, difficult Latin, the hungry student, the crawling magister, the yearned for invitation, the ob- scure post? On wobbly feet, the desk and the man, the author and his skivvy. Over them bursting rain-clouds, the stuffed shelves, paper, paper, his own writings, the used books, the old, repeated lectures, the refreshed, kempt and combed-over and pressed ideas, digests too, card-indexes, the entitled, dreamed of, feared, never hazarded work, the great questions, the unveiling, the destruction of hope, no mild age and dust dust and dust. He wears no clean nightshirt, lives on in his condemned house, his fame flowers in the annals, tended by the envy of his colleagues, eroded by the mockery of his students, as little sharp mouse teeth gnaw at the edges of folios, leaving little mouse-deposits, his nightgown, his work-clothes, bedraggled Benedictine surplice, food-spattered, shit-streaked, snuff-browned, pipe-dottle-charred, a cap over his thinning, respect-demanding hair, old fool, they say, and everywhere the vultures are peeping, whetting their beaks, signaling to the worms, the stitched silk cap a Christmas present or an anniversary gift from his wife, thirty years in bitter faithfulness, disappointed, oh, what by, uncomprehending, how could anything be different, or the daughter, looking up at him, shuddering when she looks in his face, sees her future, sees herself becoming him, and the father covers his eyes, thinks, she's growing up, the girl, twenty, thirty, and into the twilight, the orphanage for impoverished daughters of educated gentlefolk, or she will finally be handed over for academic breeding purposes to his new research assistant, a pale ambitious Judas, whom he helped to get a foothold on the ladder, introduced into the department with bowings and scrapings and little chess gambits, the presumptive falsifier and destroyer of his literary remains, the obvious betrayer of the old coryphaei, but perhaps the master is still wearing his wig, his pigtail powdered and tied à la Fritz, or already in broad-brimmed hat, silver hair well cut, shining in long locks, on the way to the Paulskirche, nearing his apotheosis, soon to be a figure of fun in the pamphlets, the man or no longer the man with the forgotten umbrella, courage, patience, in the cupboard already waits the Sedan coat, the uniform of a Lieutenant in the Reserve and all the lackey coats of his pathetic decorated decline. The ceiling presses down like a heavy hand, the window is small, as though light cost money, outside the small panes though is the idyllic arbor of jasmine and vines, that's what the heart sees, he has none, he hates it, every hour remains dark, if the sun shines then in the shadow of the tower of St. Nikolai, in fog in the sea-haar, in the washkitchen of the world, in the pincushion of creation. Homer watches the professor, his blind face propped on the baluster, or is it Pericles, the much-lauded Greek statesman with the helmet? One weak old hand quickly clutches the saving lectern, while the other trembling starts to draw the pillars, we measure with the dividers, calculate with the protractor, following the classical exemplum, the ruined temple in Athens, the shattered arch of the forum, Latin or Greek script. Mold eats away at it all. On the meadow behind the arbor they are hanging up the washing, wife, daughter, maid, perhaps they are all one and the same person, between the plum tree and the apple tree, his shirts, galley-rags, rope-belts, collars of Spanish Catholic piety, humanistic frivolity, Lutheran reform, Calvinist rigor, Loyola wiliness, his Jacobin jabots, Fichte fashions, Hegelian ribbons, gym vests, Metternich padding, stiff *Vatermörder* collars, governmental *plastrons* as stiff as breastplates, fear- and sweat-soaked huntsmen's shirts, and the cylinder for the famous seminar on the German Kaisers as executors of the will to creation and the Roman idea of the world-empire, with long underpants for excursions on the heath, the sites of our German-Wendtish bones, and also the home economy patched and turned sheets, the maternally plumped featherbeds for nocturnal revival, he lies alone, a single professor in the nest warmth of sweat and the decomposing flesh of the gradually dissolving spouse, decomposition from the very first day, from the hour of recognition, he didn't look, didn't look at his own body as time gnawed it, at night the mind visited him, came with the owl of Minerva, came from the Temple of Ephesus, temple-servants gave themselves to him, the stranger, the exile, the dreamer, but he stayed true to his dream glory be to god in the highest, it was just a screech-owl screaming too-whit-too-whoo, the bone man, or came to him the ideas, the birth of the nation, the people rose up, but the storm was not unleashed, the flaming sword bred for throne and altar, the preserves waited in jars and pots in the cellar, for someone to fall ill, from the ropewalk he hears the rasp of the ropeman's wheel, the dead in their graves in Etruria, led by the hemp-weaver, protected in the underworld, and the mason comes and gets the plan, and mixes the white sand with mortar, and the carpenter nails together the scaffold and the mold and the coffin, at noon the town smells of frying flounders, in the evening of smoked fish from Susemihl's emporium, and there isn't enough money to go round, and the town tires of so much sublimity, the town fathers say, with all respect, two pillars will do, Caesar and Alexander have not been forgotten here in Greifswald, but the heavy gable, the sarcophagus of stone blocks, the Huns' grave that contains nothing and no one but the myth of a great ancestor, they lie heavy either side of the gate on their true supports, unseen, squat gray pedestals of common clay.

the park in Putbus and in the background the castle of the Duke of Putbus, and the castle looks exactly like the castle of the Duke of Putbus the way it is on the picture postcards that they sell at the entrance to the park, ten pfennigs for the black and white, or strictly speaking fog and gray realistic version, and twenty for the white castle under an azure almost tropical sky on an emerald green lawn. The castle is neither big nor small, it looks dazzling in its new whitewash, it is a pretty white castle, and in the context of Rügen or Pomerania, it is Versailles or Sans Souci or something like that. On the black slate roof of the castle flies the Duke's flag, the schoolmaster of Putbus says His Excellency's banner is hoisted, the spa visitors whisper to one another, the Duke's at home. What do the spa visitors know? The Duke is dining off golden plates, the Duke's crown is sewn into the tablecloth, the Duke's coat of arms is blazoned on the china and the heavy silver, the Duke rules, but over whom does he rule? The Duke is asleep, he is embracing his Duchess, he is breeding the next Duke of Putbus, who will not rule, who will fall, murdered in the snow, buried in the desert sand, put under the ice in the fjord, lowered into the depth of the ocean. The old Duke has a mistress and breeds a writer or a minister or a revolutionary or a hotel owner, but some of the locals say, our Duke is dead. The park is laid out in accordance with English principles, the Duke or Duchess or their ancestors or the architect they commissioned or cheated, or someone who had their ear, a whisperer, a flatterer, a property speculator, perhaps a bona fide Englishman, a homosexual and an émigré repressing or cultivating tender memories of Hyde Park, perhaps some boy with girlish complexion, or a boyish-featured milk-maid dropped on the trim rain-slicked lawn and forgotten or never forgotten—they all loved, and above all they loved nature. Deer were supposed to graze in the wide clearings. And deer did graze there, and trustingly drew near, taking stale bread from the hands of their enemies, snuffling and nuzzling the extended self-satisfied hand, but nowadays you don't see any deer, the deer are gone, stolen, hunted down, shot with army rifles, killed by hand grenades, slaughtered by night, perhaps the Duke ate them all, while the banner of His Grace's presence rippled on the roof, or perhaps others ate the deer, stuffed themselves on venison, while the Duke sat at his laid table, in front of empty golden plates in the gala room without a fire and without light, and listened to the shots, the detonations of hand grenades in front of his house, in his park, among his deer, whom he loved and did not want to slaughter, and perhaps all this happened even as the Duke was dying. The paths in the park are all lovingly sprinkled with sand, brought in on the Baltic waves, carted there by laborers, and it all looks very tidy. The sand is white and fine, washed by the sea, occasionally a piece of shell crunches underfoot, and there's always an old man who looks like the Duke and is perhaps his brother, busy raking the paths. In season at any rate. My mother is sitting on a bench in the park that was put there by the Castle administration or the spa. My mother is writing. She isn't writing postcards, she isn't sending the Duke of Putbus's castle home or into the wide world somewhere. No holiday greetings or wish-you-were-heres. On her knees she has a worn book, a collection of fingerprints, memories of irregular, carelessly eaten meals, burn-marks from glumly smoked cigarettes, the piano score of a comic opera, and on the tatty old piano score is a sheet of yellow office paper that my mother found somewhere or picked up, and it's me she's writing to: starve if that's what you want to do, if you're so wicked as to do that to me, I can't help you if you won't help yourself, and she takes the plunge and writes, you know God helps those who help themselves, and it's the God of Luther and the little catechism and his faithfully procreating preachers subject to authority, and she looks up at the sky and she knows that this is all a sigh of helplessness, dictation taken from another's hand, another's mouth, a puff of chill. The spa visitors stroll up and down the paths, as it's what they've come to do. The women's skirts are short following the late war, they stop just below the knee, which is a new and shocking development, a sign of degen-

eration, proof that the world is coming to an end, and the old
Duchess of Putbus does not participate in the fashion, her skirts
and underskirts always brush the sand, leaving unmistakable sign
that she has passed this way, as once in Potsdam when she was
maid-of-honor to the Empress or at the Court of the Tsarina, who
is no more, engulfed by a whirlpool, eaten up by a monster, and
the men showed some dignity then still, heads held high, stiff collars, gold chains across their bellies, and all their unmentionables
safely stowed away under their swallowtail coats as in a sack, striding upright into the future, which, incredibly distant and inex-
pressibly filthy, visible only to Cassandra, concealed the grave in a
proud dazzle, the great new charnel houses. My mother is still
young. Her skirt too has been taken up. My grandmother would
not have approved. The skirt is crumpled and threadbare, it's
made out of a cheap pawky cloth, *ersatz* cloth, perhaps woven out
of stinging nettles, an invention of the great epoch and perhaps its
survivor. My mother's gray worsted stockings are holey; some
holes have been darned, there wasn't the thread or the time for the
rest. My mother's shoes are down at heel, and her soles have gaping holes. The collar and cuffs of my mother's blouse are dirty. My
mother owns no second blouse. Sometimes she washes the blouse
in the bowl on the washstand of her little room with the fisherman's wife (the fisherman, hopeful of halibut, stayed behind in
Skagerrak), but my mother can't always be washing her one
blouse. She too is running out of time. Art claims her. But it isn't
art, so much as destiny. My mother's face is as white as snow, as
red as blood, and as black as ebony, frozen and scraped like the
skin on Dr. Oetker's ambrosia pudding made with skim milk, my
mother is harried, she's about to fall, she can feel it, she's reached
her limit. Death is hiding behind the tree, neither friend nor foe,
an official, a bag of bones. My mother has had to do the rounds
of many government offices. Her hand, guiding the pencil stub
over the yellow office paper and wanting to send me to the perdi-
tion that she cannot master, is trembling. My mother is sitting in
a cage. A small cage. It has three walls and the three walls shut her
in. There is no fourth wall. The air in the cage is redolent of wood
shavings, of carpenter's glue, of unprimed canvas and acrid oil

paint, and above all of dust. The air smells of hot feet in shoes too stout for the time of year, and worn too long. The much-touted blue sky of the summer visitors is nowhere to be seen. The beautiful Baltic is nowhere to be seen either. The only sign of summer is the heat, which falls heavily into the basement, into the cage where my mother is kept penned. A lamp shines in her face. My mother leans forward out of her cage and whispers; but in a whisper that is a tense shout couched in a whisper. My mother is sitting in the prompters' box of the Ducal Putbus Summer Theater, and reads the piano score out loud, and speaks the words of the comic opera in a vigorous whisper. The singers haven't learned their parts. They are, as they say, floundering. Silent fish. Silent, dusty varnished aquarium. From my mother's point of view, as she peers out over the piano score, there are only feet in view, dusty damp poor feet. Only when my mother looks up at the singers, and gives them a helpful prompt, the word long waited for, the droll word that sets things going again, does she see the faces of the actors. Hungry, furious, relentless faces; demanding nothing less than my mother's life. Because they too, unfortunates, are formed of clay, and demand to be brought to life by being breathed upon. Their expression is lordly, arrogant, conceited, reproachful, the singers' faces are accusations, because their ears or their memory or their mind fail to grasp or are unable to grasp the lines my mother whispers or shouts to them. The singers open their mouths, but not to sing with; they forget to close their mouths, which do not sing; my mother looks into black hollows of imbecility, and the eyes of the singers wander or pierce, are perplexed or angry. The rehearsal drags on. Far up in the sky, a storm is gathering. The director scolds, he is sleeping with the starlet, so he doesn't scold the starlet, the old bed creaks, the fisherman's widow and landlady listens behind the thin wooden wall and gets aroused, the oppressive featherbed is pushed back from sweating limbs, it's a close night in the attic, whoever has visited the tropics or read about the tropics might think: forest of lianas, flicker of summer lightning, a pig is grunting in the widow's little sty, snuffling truffling around in the starlet's damp body, the well-spring under wet moss, musty air as in a tomb, missed the cue, death-white powdered face, little runnels of panic and heat, no understanding, of course not, where would understanding come from? The director doesn't scold the singers, all colleagues at cards, the third deals, the kibitzers watch, they know it all, happy to be treated to a short, and then a beer to follow, what manner of men are they in their trousers, ex-soldiers, served with distinction in the Baltic, no, in the front theater, the director's scolding voice is directed down at my mother, whoever is poor will sit down way down, and shall be raised, said Pastor Buttentien, the Court Chaplain at Putbus, the director hops up in the air, truly, God is raising him up, now he's playing the fool, he's skipping around, belly swaying, now everyone's in a line, linking arms, the universe has been returned to its limits, legs kicking up, forward to the edge of the stage, red, haloes from the flies. The grand giddy finale, love, oh love, is sent us from above

he went to the station as it got dark, or in the dark if it was winter, went to meet the eight o'clock train from Berlin, hurried to get there early, wandered around the station like a bum, climbed up on the bridge from which one could look down on the rails that went to Scandinavia, Malmo, Stockholm or Pasewalk, or to Stettin or Berlin, or where the trains were shunted back and forth, a locomotive pushed or pulled, moved off, the goods carriages banged against the buffers, their brakes screaked, potatoes on open goods wagons, or sugar-beets or corn or livestock in covered wagons peering out through the barred carriages into this eve of departure that was warm or chill, and if chill then he could see the animals' breath, the damp nostrils of the cows, their rosy muzzles, the nostrils through which they snuffed the smoky air of the station, said goodbye to the pastures the grass the wind the limitless view of the sea into the foggy world, bound for Berlin, its big appetite, greedy to consume them, gentle cattle, clever pigs, doomed from birth, and on the other side of the station, where the track led past fences behind which was nothing or just rubbish dreck a patch of dry earth a collapsed garden hut and then shining into the night out of high windows or open windows, from little windows, from the opened or barred windows of the

psychiatric clinic, the nuthouse, he stood above the locomotives'
smoke, sooting up, becoming steambound, it was only the little
train to Stralsund, he climbed down the steps back into the station, he went into the station hall, cautiously, looked to see if the
policeman was lurking, the plainclothesman in his cloak, with his
hunting hat, saw the other lads who hung around here, also looking out for the policeman, for enemies, clipes, illiterates, he went
over to the newspaper stand, looked them over, had no money, the Berlin papers were coming on the eight o'clock train, he
asked about any leftovers from the day before, was given them or
not, with the masthead torn off, for pennies, which he paid or for
which he owed, then the express rolled in, and there they came,
he stood behind the barrier and stared at them, not the businessmen with the sample cases that were as big as he was, they were
expected by hotel messengers, were taken on to the Nordischer Hof or the Preussischer Hof or the Black Eagle, he was spec-
ulating on those passengers who were coming to visit the town
for reasons unknown, who were struggling with heavy suitcases,
but not heavy enough to have had them shipped separately, who
didn't know yet what hotel they were headed for, or who wanted to take a look around before going anywhere, and he peered
at the policeman, trotted along next to the travellers, addressed
them, whispered humbly, offered to carry their respected suitcases for them, the other lads shouldered him aside, tripped him up,
barged him, hit him, but he found gaps, he was quicker, or the
others were distracted by other quarry, and the traveller hesitated,
looked at him, scrutinized him, and before the traveller could say
no, he grabbed the suitcase handle, twisted it out of the visitor's
hand, picked up the suitcase, hoisted it onto his shoulder, stag-
gering a little under the weight, and carried it walking along beside the visitor, they crossed over the Wall, he led the way, if the
visitor was a stranger here, he described the town to him, he said,
this is where Nachtigall the African explorer lived, and the visitor
had heard of Nachtigall, or he hadn't heard of him, and the visitor didn't care much either way, and the lad imagined he was the
traveller, Nachtigall, back from Africa with a suitcase full of ivory or full of gold, but Nachtigall had died in poverty, though he

was a professor, but he was a rich Herr Nachtigall as he crossed the market square to the Nordischer Hof, he strode casually down the red carpet, carrying his suitcase stuffed with Africa's gold, with Africa's ivory, with the tusks of Africa's elephants, the spotted fur of its leopards, and he tossed the porter a mark or even two, or he gave him a dollar and ordered a room in the *bel étage*, facing the street naturally, and he ordered fried flounders up in his room or the roast goose stuffed with apples and prunes, and the traveller pressed thirty pfennigs into his hand or maybe fifty, and the hotel porter came up in his green apron, grabbed the suitcase and shouted, clear off. Get out and stay out.

The courthouse was built of brick, and it shone summer and winter, slick with rain, or in sunlight or by lamplight. Its popular old German boxy style of 1870 was evocative of south German towns, a folksy romanticism that I knew from paintings, the façade, with a hint of Renaissance, of palaces and prisons. Inside, the court was a bewildering confusion of organization, guarded by Prussian officials, poorly remunerated NCOs, something for Franz Kafka of Prague to have described, whom I then didn't know and who later colored my memory, or for Piranesi to have drawn, whom I loved. I lost my way in panic, ran madly up and down stairs. I was looking for a door through which I could flee. I had been accused, who by, by everyone, not of anything in particular, or else the Court of Chancery had found me in their files, accused of being alive. Power loomed, stood in front of the house, its purposes inscrutable. My mother and I wondered if we should play dead, ignore the summons, draw the curtains to keep out the town. We were a closed society of our own, on occasion stand-offish. We lay in our beds at right angles to each other, not sleeping. We did nothing but listen to the other's breathing; sensing it might stop at any moment, out of fury or fatigue. At the back of the court, towards the Kastanienwall, the prison was connected to the court, one body, and perhaps also one soul. Prisoners in their cells looked through the bars out on to the Wall, at the pedestrians under the chestnuts, at my mother and me, at the red clay courts of the University Tennis Club and its educated forehands.

In the fine weather, the striking of the balls was the bastinado of the upper crust, for the benefit of the inmates. When it was winter, the snow pretended to level things between the privileged and the unprivileged. But when I found out that Aunt Martha was a judge in the family court, I went to him, without informing my mother, driven by curiosity to meet such a judge, to see him and speak to him, to see him go about his work.

Aunt Martha was a well-known figure in the town, and had long been one of those people who intrigued me, whom I secretly tailed, whom I tried to imagine being, so that I could understand them and dream their dreams for them. Aunt Martha was a senior judge at the local assizes. It had taken a lot for the town to get used to him, and even now it winced. As a long-serving senior official he was tolerated, which certain dogmatic characters thought was a scandal. Malicious students had come up with the name Aunt Martha, and the citizens with their insatiable appetite for disorder had avidly taken it up. Aunt Martha was tall and bony, with a long puppet's nose and deep-lying sad eyes in masses of wrinkles. If he raised his eyelids, his eyes seemed to peep out as from a tortoise's carapace. I saw him on the street, bent over, files under his arm, bowing, scraping, being humiliated. A smile of inborn kindness and shocking embarrassment stretched his features. Unhealed wounds in his face hurt me. He teetered along with brisk ladies' steps through the sore air of the courthouse. He held his right hand as though lifting a trailing skirt out of the dirt. He sat at home, rumor had it from various ill-intentioned sources, in sleeveless outfits from some pre-War fashion journal, scooped out in front and back, at a knitting frame and conjured beautiful bouquets of wool or yarn. I didn't like those stories. They made me furious. I imagined him instead residing in an inherited villa behind the old cemetery, living among books, a cat on his lap, reading Plato. I envied him. I wanted to ask him to teach me Greek. I had a grammar and a dictionary, and I left Greek scribbles on the edges of newspapers, and read the Classical poets in the antique translations of the German Hellenophiles, the idealists and humanists of yore. On the court steps, I imitated Aunt Martha, teetered after him in his manner, raised the imaginary skirt, it wasn't with any evil intention, I wanted to be able to read his thoughts, and so I copied him. Aunt Martha was the public representative of morality and its laws. The question was: was he a hypocrite? I didn't think so. Only something had broken inside him in this town, he found himself and his desires a little frivolous, or perhaps celibacy had made him wise, like an old priest. So I came to stand before him, and in files, reports, and denunciations from the gutter or from people's best rooms, it said I was a rebel. Against whom, and where to begin, and why not? Aunt Martha had been given power, he would have been able to kill, he was the overlord of various institutions, ruinous torture-chambers for children in the sticks, but kind-hearted and sympathetic to young people and not without doubt regarding the law and public morality as a whole, asserting his friendliness, his insight and his sorrow in the teeth of the severity that was expected of him. I liked all that, and it disposed me to trust him. Since all the world made fun of Aunt Martha, the child did not mock him. That was too much for the judge. My file was left lying, it dropped into the oubliettes of the building. In the end it was encased in spiders' webs and forgotten by time, which could on occasion be merciful.

The Deutsche Lichtspiele had always drawn me, with its long passageway looking half-asleep by day, and festively lit in the evenings and on Sunday afternoons, with its black noticeboards announcing the joys to come, the advertising displays, the stills from the features, the never previously seen and quite unattainable beings in tempting shining worlds of wealth, pleasure, distance, excess and adventure, also of pain and danger, a universe of fate and guile, full of traps and temptations, violent early death, but also generous triumphs and gifts from the gods. The garish placards beckoned with impossible close-ups of loving or dying mouths, or the dagger plunged into the heaving, ripped and bloody bosom. The program changed every Tuesday and Friday, with different announcements and exhibits, and I went there and took it all in and saw myself pursued, and finally prevailed, I leaped onto moving trains, or off industrial chimneys into the baskets of hap-

pening-by balloons, I fought Indians, conquered foreign coun-
tries, rescued fair women and asked for no thanks, in order, as a
ghost in ancient castles, to pull the white booty from the four-
poster bed, to be lucky, to win millions and gold, to go to the
scaffold with a puckish smile on my face. Greedily I breathed in
the rather used air that came through the black dust-sheet that
separated the cinema auditorium from the passage and the little
rococo cage of the box office. Sometimes my desire to see what
was going on in the night so magically lit up by the projector's
beam was so strong that I stole money from my mother, scrab-
bled together the apparel of a grown man from various yards and
attics, a stiff collar, an armor-thick ironed shirt-front, a beaten-
up bowler hat, in order to present myself in disguise at the black
and white paradise that was off-limits to the young. Then I became the prisoner of the cinema, Herr Segebracht, the owner of
the Deutsche Lichtspiele, had taken me on on my application, to
usher patrons to their seats, and to run errands for the business.
No one asked me any more whether I was old enough to disappear behind the black dust-cloth and serve the shadows. I no longer needed to bother with my costume. In the evening I hurried along with my torch, whose battery I was instructed by Herr
Segebracht to preserve as much as possible, through the dim rows
of seats, like Ariadne, leading the way through the labyrinth. But
Theseus was dead, I had never forgotten him, he had introduced
me to this exciting world of shadowplay, I was six or seven, the
war had begun, and Theseus was our furnished lodger, though of
scant respect, not a real lodger, not a student, much less a lectur-
er, merely a temporary salesman in Erdmann's department store,
fabrics section, we had visited him there, I had seen him in front
of his counter with tape-measure in hand, like the rapier wield-
ing fraternity student, ready to run through an imaginary enemy,
a hero like Siegfried, but no one but me had noticed or understood that he was a hero, and about to face the Minotaur. One
evening he knocked softly on our door and asked if he could take
me to the Deutsche Lichtspiele, and my mother hadn't wanted to
allow it, and I had begged and cried, because the Deutsche Lichtspiele seemed to me like a temple, the most tempting thing in the

world, the shrine of truth, the explanation of everything that zealous adults tried to keep from me, and the fact that Theseus wanted to take me there was the unhoped for stroke of fate, the decisive lucky break of fairy-tales, it was the chance, offered only to me and never again, to be initiated, and even if I didn't have Pastor Koch's theological armor, I did feel I would be eating of the fruit of the Tree of Knowledge. Theseus asked my mother to let me go with him, he was lonely, it was his last evening, he had just received his call-up, and my mother looked at him, and I don't know if she saw him disappear as he stood before her, dissolve, simply cease to exist, and air press in to where he had stood, air replace him as though he had never been, and he took me by the hand and walked with me to the Deutsche Lichtspiele. We strode through the shining gates, walked down the auspicious passage, and Theseus bought two tickets for the box on his last evening in our town, where he had worked selling silk and fustian and other stuffs, and sat down with me, a child, that was astonished by everything, and for the first time saw reality in darkness, in the boxy enclosure of the box, at the very back of the cinema. Before long we were both admiring a big wide commanding man by the name of Hindenburg and a thousand or for all I know a hundred thousand fleeing Russians, insect-like gray swarms fleeing into the Masurian swamps, and a hand, a magic hand, appeared on the shining screen, it was holding a pen, and it deftly and quickly drew the Kaiser with eagle helmet and eagle eye and curled as it were flashing tips of his moustaches in redoubtable bronze and top-boots, and with those shining polished spurred top-boots he kicked some pathetic figures who were our enemies, and were Serbs and Russians and French and Brits, in the panic-stricken seat of their pants, which they then clutched, wailing and in low impotent rage.

Then there appeared on the screen, transmitted by the beam and the dusty Milky Way from the projectionist's box, aptly enough, but in a different scene or setting, Death. With shouldered scythe, Civilian Death strode with farmer-like calm over a field, that was well-planted, fertile, and no field of battle. In spite of his mower's blade, Death calmly striding over the field was like the familiar figure of the sower in the parable of that name. He wore a black slouch hat like Pastor Koch did when he looked in on us to remonstrate with us; only the bony face of Death looked friendlier than Pastor Koch's double chin. That night I had nightmares. My mother sat on my bed and held me tight while I thrashed about and screamed. A new word had just appeared in the world that was used liberally and almost reverently, namely the word war widow, and I saw my mother, dressed in black, sitting bent over a notification of death. Who was I fighting against in my night? Even by morning, it wasn't Death that I remembered, only the Kaiser in his pomp and strength, and soon after my mother told me Theseus had fallen. He had left me behind in the labyrinth of new-fangled flickering shadows, in their soon everyday shower. The shadows did not weep for Theseus. A servant of the Minotaur, who sometimes took himself for Ariadne, I watched the shadows two or three times a day, and came to see through them in their stereotypical repetitions. I saw the comedy figures meet, run around together, fall in love, be deceived, hate one another, pursue one another in desire or fear, fail to shrink from crime, even murder, until in the end in the halo of the last yards of the film a man and a woman, a hero and heroine, a couple with a chance of stabilizing their true false feelings, of stability and babies, fell into each other's arms. Of all the other people who had surrounded them, advanced them in their plot, caused them joy and sorrow, laid obstacles across their path, or perhaps merely been kind to them, there was no more mention, their death and their sacrifice was futile and justified by the happiness of a higher class of shadow. Arm in arm, mouth to mouth, the male and female stars clung together in their two dimensions, the trademark of one Mr. William Fox who had been honored to present them.

The lads at the station, the little hungry porters, the quarrelsome tourist guides I tried to steer clear of, the obedient middle class children at school, whom I hadn't liked, and whose company I sadly or tempestuously quit, sought me out in the Deutsche Lichtspiele like ghosts, insolent or shy, and I, a trusted holder of an office, a guardian of Hades, secretly let them through the black curtain into the dark mystery across the Styx. In return, they had to wrestle with me. Following cops and robbers and cowboy films, following comedies and dramas not open to children, we went into the cinema yard to the rubbish bins stuffed with ripped down posters flapping in the wind, and stripped for bad fights, that were not without the desire to feel pain, to feel the muscles of the other, to hear the heart in his boy's breast beat against mine, to suck in his hot breath. One afternoon Fräulein von Lossin visited our cinema. We were showing a film about Fridericus Rex that was very popular and which the town liked very much, Frederick's victories were ours, his defeats forgotten, he was a Prussian, can you name his colors, the students came in hordes and cheered, and Fräulein von Lossin sat in the box at the back, where I had sat with Theseus when I was a boy and watched as the enemy were beaten and chased into the swamps. I was still ashamed of my humiliation, and hid, and made myself small, I tried with my torch to dazzle Fräulein von Lossin, and keep myself in the dark. I didn't know at the time that she, whom I assumed was sunning herself in the glory of the king and the war, was grieving for a man murdered and buried behind the Huns' grave in the woods belonging to her former estate. I followed her persistently, not because she was involved in Vehmic reprisals, but I trailed her though the streets, concealed myself in entryways, used the dusk; I don't know why. It didn't bother me, but it somehow touched me that she or her family were living on the estate, owned the estate that following my mother's stories had belonged to my grandmother. For a long time I had the notion that I was in love with Fräulein von Lossin, I liked the idea, I felt love in my bed, I rescued her from burning barns, from capsized boats, from ice floes, pulled her off wild mustangs, asking for no recompense, neither the estate nor her, who was worshipped by haughty fraternity students, the brute sons of a shocked society. On one occasion I followed her and her green-capped escort into a university department, expecting them to begin kissing, which duly happened in front of a tall glass case in which rabbits and mice were fed to big snakes in a sealed space from which they could not flee, but in which they seemed to show no fear, either didn't sense or didn't understand the proximity of their end, behaved perfectly normally, without horror, yes, even groomed themselves in the coils of the snake, showing neither disgust nor panic. Only when Fräulein von Lossin, sixteen years old, happened to catch sight of me, whom she didn't know, at most recognizing in me her unworthy pursuer through the glass case of the nightmarish death, she was startled and pushed the green-capped student away.

The funeral procession passed through the Lange Strasse, twelve coffins laid on a lorry, and one that stood in for all on the bier, with horses in black trappings and black ribbons on the traces, the dead man lay as in a black four-poster and on him, as on all the others in the lorry, the wreaths with red ribbons, the comrades for the comrades, the town funeral band played the tune 'Unforgotten Victims,' and they trotted along after in silence unarmed not even carrying sticks, only a few with flags, the red stitched and embroidered flags of the trade unions, the pavements of the Lange Strasse were empty, the shops were shuttered, there was no sign of those in colors, the temporary volunteers, the Black and other Reichswehr, the Kapp militias with their death's head, and the others from the Baltic with their swastikas.

The next day the street was full of strollers, schoolboys and schoolgirls from the Augusta Victoria Lyceum had blackwhitered ribbons pinned on, the students came out in their fraternity colors, all the shops were open, the shopkeepers were smiling, with muffled drumroll they were burying a temporary volunteer killed by a ricochet, and the Reichswehr followed with a guard of honor, the students followed, and the Provost of the University in full regalia.

They had dashed his brains out, they had dashed his brains out in the forest, he had cried for help, or perhaps he hadn't cried for help, because he knew all ears were deaf, and one of them had a shovel, a short-handled field-shovel, the weapon that had caught out the generals, with which the generals had proved unable to deal, that had decided the outcome of the war one way or another, they carried the field-shovel on their belt, they liked carrying the field-shovel on their belt, even when they were no longer obliged to carry the field-shovel on their belt or anywhere else, and they would have been able to go if they'd wanted, they could have dispersed, left the banner, which had long since ceased to exist, left the forced community, the regiment of death, but they had no desire to disperse, to leave their community, to leave death and commands, they were afraid their bodies might be lost to them in freedom, conjured away, suddenly not be there, they needed a belt round their waists and a stout buckle with God for King and Fatherland or just with God on our side, and one of them swung at him from behind with the spade, they had let him go on ahead, they were trotting through the forest, and the man struck him flush on the back of the head, and he fell, fell to the forest floor, fell on the oak leaves the linden leaves the beech leaves the birch leaves, he had a taste of bitter moss in his mouth, and maybe he was someone who liked cress with his carp or his halibut, if he had gone on to take Holy Orders as he had wanted to take Holy Orders, on Good Friday or at Christmas following the Holy Supper after the sermon, and then they turned him on to his back, and kicked him with their hobnailed boots that had marched back from Verdun, Brest-Litovsk and Gallipoli, they marched forward on their nailed boots into his guts, they crushed his ribs, stamped the marching nails of their jack-boots in his eyes, drilled their steel toecaps in his split skull, finally they saw what they wanted to see, his brain, they didn't understand, didn't get it, looked stupidly down at the gray mass, at the detritus of a human being, who had had what they weren't blessed with, singularity, mind, a heart, a tongue to speak with, the belief in an immortal soul, who had been courageous, not only at Verdun and not only to order, who had been pained by death where he saw it, who had been wounded, visibly and invisibly, and who had stored within him the treasures of our common inheritance, the libraries of Ephesus, of Babylon, of Alexandria, the Sermon on the Mount, who had talked about the freedom of a Christian in a rectory, the human rights of people all over the world, Latin, Greek and Hebrew, Tolstoy in the blizzard, a poor peasant in Yasnaya Polnaya, and the distant storm of the *O Mensch* cries at Berlin artists' cafés, and then they buried him, what else did they have spades for, they dug a hole for him with their bloodied shovels, a shallow one, what did they have to be afraid of, though they cursed the roots of trees that got in their way, they hacked with their shovels at the spreading roots, they gave his corpse one last kick into the ditch, and they covered him over. Here was a Huns' grave. A fox found his carcass. Or a boar. There wasn't much meat on him.

He lay buried in the woods until they dug him up and laid him out on a gurney in the anatomy department, on the yucky rubber sheet, the damp, squamous skin of a frog, on the algal smooth goose-bump-making battered sheath of a snake or other reptile that had appalled him when they shoved a skink in his satchel, or a newt or salamander, and the laughter that followed when he reached for his history book, the victories, the defeats, the kings and all the many many dead, and the anatomy janitor rinsed the cloth with a spray from his hose, the way he sprayed the execution place clean in prison, his sideline, after the judgment, after the prayer, after the execution, that followed the well-thought-out procedures of the Imperial-Republican for executions, following a protocol like that for royal visits, not those of presidents, brushed shining top hats were the pride of spouses, awoke memories of the marriage altar and the awful bedded wife and the hope for a seemly funeral, orders showed that you were someone to be reckoned with and not to be reckoned with, basically that you sat at the top table, and remained in power and defied all your enemies, a servant to your superiors, or that you had at least a share of power, they had flint faces wily comprehensively greedy deceitful faces, sprays the blood, swills away the excreta, along with the sympathy that shyly choked you, and into the stinking chlorinated cloaca with the commandment thou shalt not kill, to which they appealed as they swung the axe, and they opened the body, inasmuch as it wasn't already gaping, their rubber hands and their scalpels tinkered and tooled away, they want-

ed to learn, learn more, with beating heart, I hope, under the
rubber apron, beating covertly, they themselves couldn't hear it,
it was swaddled tight in elevating feelings, it was armor-plated
by false history, it was, they praised it themselves, a heart of gun-
metal and shell steel and, as they and their fathers thought, proof
against temptations that might yet come, one day, at some un-
foreseen hour of day or night, after the first sleep, or at noon,
when food and beer had made you drowsy, the heart was isolated
from the stream of the world, withdrawn from a feeling of broth-
erhood that ought to exist, they learned from him who was now
colder than the froggy undersheet than the clammy rubber skin
pulled over their hands than the rigid rubber apron, more unfeel-
ing under their knives than the cool blades, they learned quickly
not to take on so if they wanted to get on in life, and they wanted
to get on, not like him, and they agreed that one oughtn't to be
like him, they were satisfied that he had come to such a bad end,
because they sympathized openly with his killers, assiduous students of medicine, student doctors of forensic science, trainees,
escapees who didn't know how to escape, and who felt at a dis-
advantage vis-à-vis the dead man, they preferred field gray tunics
to narrow or tight civilian pants or field gray baggy breeches, the
seat reinforced with leather, sweated through and worn to a shine,
and the horse was dead, had remained behind on the expedition
a mangled mess, or the horse had always been just a dream, muf-
ti suits in their cupboards, or those inherited from brothers who
would never rise from the dead, veterans come home from the
war, survivors from the killing fields beyond the horizon, ghosts
of the dead man, crawled back to the fatherland, lulled by the fa-
therlie, absorbed into the fatherguilt, co-responsible, volunteers
as ever, toughened, enraged, but enraged with whom, they looked
back on so many dead that they failed to see how dead the survivors were or those who had never been in jeopardy, the oldsters
who had won again, who had sent them out to meet their deaths,
and they crawled to the Cross, and were unaware of their humiliation, tired of futility, tired of life, not tired of death, a match
for everything but not for the truth, defeated (though not in battle) and to the end of their lives stunned by empty singing, by

parping hollow trumpets, by bonging hollow drums, by stupid proud words, the windy teachers who had made them suffer, it had come off, it had been done, now they believed in that world of their elders, which they had not defended but yet supported, they stooped greedily under the yoke from which they had set out in their *Wandervogel* kit on the road to Langemarck, fraternity boys, corps brothers, they thought: sonofabitch, they thought this is his body, they examined what was before them, what was left of him, for now, were duly disgusted, felt like a beer, bottoms up, and the head the boss the old man of the corps or the fraternity and its youthful ribbons dry stick thought as they did: only fair, and he brought them up in accordance with his great hero, little baby chiefs, if they were lucky and behaved themselves and remained subservient to the true, indestructible power, which might change its face but never its views, and the preceptor thought: only fair, and he was bowing and scraping to become chief himself, and they were full of contempt for the dead man and full of zeal for the living, they crossly wrote out the verdict, which the state prosecutor, of the same mind as themselves, crossly received, they didn't put his skeleton in a glass case for their collection, he had too many broken bones, too much shot up busted cartilage which the Iron Cross had covered, it was doing him too much honor, but whoever wanted an arm or a jawbone took it home with them, laid it on the walnut inlaid desk in the furnished lodgings under the blackwhitered or the *Stahlhelm* or the swastika banner, and let it gather dust.

I heard the shots, the hand grenades going off in the distance, over streets and courtyards, gabled roofs, town gardens with flowers and fruit trees, the echo rolled, broke against the sky, dropped like a canopy, crashing over my bed; there was fighting in the marketplace, fighting in the Lange Strasse, fighting in the paupers' cottages, a last stand in front of the trade union house, and they lost.

The young lady had had her picture taken in the photographic atelier, in the glass canopy under the sky, the dingy white curtains adjusted light and shade, the maestro crawled under the black cloth bag, saw the beauty standing on her head, moved his wood and brass box nearer, saw her in sharp focus, let the little birdie out, she hung with cherries by her swelling lips in a glass vitrine, with clouds behind her, frozen among the newlyweds in dread of matrimony, among the confirmands in their old man suits, their too-wide starched collars, a black pallbearer's hat in their hands in an effort to hide them, the penis idling stiffly in their scratchy pants.

Hand grenades had blown up the atelier, and in the window-displays behind the shards of broken glass they had torn away parts of the models, some had lost an arm or a head, and the girl had lost some of her mouth, so that the cherries suspended between the parted lips looked as though they were jammed in a wound, and transformed what had been a playful set-up into one suggesting torture.

The pictures of actors on a carton in the window of the cigar store: the man in evening cape, the white silk lining draped like batwing, the monocle in his eye, the top hat at an angle, a gold- or silver-headed cane ready to beat time or smash skulls.

The passage with its reddish lino floor still damp from the mop smelled of petroleum and carbolic flammable air he ran through in green-yellow blue-red iris flowering plant the tickle ran up his leg the fire door was not locked led out to the roof space of the town hall dancenight balletnight musicnight the stars of film and broadcast reverend direction of the Berlin Hillermillerziller revue a thousand sweet leggy girls in the big city hall on the speaker's podium of patriotic songs in the attic the wardrobes he bent down humiliated himself as he knew gave in surrendered to God's will he shot a glance round peeped through the keyhole of the locked door saw the line of make-up tables the mirrors the light-bulbs the mirrors had captured little moons parts of bodies slippery sateen he smelled the dropped slips the lacy chemises pulled over the head the bustiers the brassieres and stockings laid over

the arms of brewery chairs fallen on the ground they sat stretched
kicked picked up garments with their bare feet the tutus and glit-
ter the Berlin girls naked to the sanitary pad the packaging stress-
ing the sex their menstrual rags cut into his groin he thought of
the hair matted under muslin and gauze he had never seen them
in the flesh wet with blood and juice and lacquer on the wet va-
gina in Döderlein's Gynecological Atlas in the university library
open in the reading room borrowed from the one-handed refer-
ence section the medical shelf on the gray iron gallery holed steps
noisy plates underfoot Döderlein knew what was what, saw the
female animal healthy or (more usually) diseased pinned open the
labia left nothing unbared the heaving belly the uterine shrimp
or even a baby tumbling into the world head first ancient head
mewling no doubt or the first cry of shock or even gripped in the
midwife's forceps the skull heaving chopping and one more citizen no cretin no genius maybe an irritation a stammerer pre- or
peri-natal trauma and in front of the keyhole in the door his eye
and behind the door the other side of the keyhole the Berlin girls
their thick short thighs their thin scrawny backstairs legs rickety
lumps on the joints the so-called English disease war hunger and
years in bomb shelters but the skin white average age twenty maybe they powdered their flesh the powder puff passed over their
protuberant bellies a dab of rouge on the nipples or they rubbed
themselves screeching giggling touched themselves sang komm
mein Lieschen Lieschen Lieschen page-boy cuts porcelain dolls
with bleached marcelled hair already brittle stuck in the comb
was teased out covered the floor stuck to their bare soles water
roared toilet flush the sound drilled into your neck ran down your
spine toughness dissolved pain like a sharp knife sliced behind the
forehead the eyes tired the bell pealed in the henyard performance
of the thousand legs parade of Berliner Luft Luft Luft he ran
back down the corridor through the fire door the emergency exit
reached the city theater the beginners' wardrobe the small players
mirrors sweat and Leichner's greasy make-up Göbel stood there
in his long underwear he disdained Göbel long foot long toes
aroused phallus you have to wash yourself every day from head
to toe even if it be in a tin bucket that's the least a girl can expect

Göbel saw it as a question of hygiene his black parting gleamed coaxingly a crooked pretty smile he was successful with the ladies he cut a swathe through them he didn't care if they could speak were young and beautiful or not

On other evenings I went to the theater. When my mother wasn't too depressed, she called me a stage-door Johnnie. It must have been an expression she had picked up from a book somewhere, and she always used it mockingly, but also with a little surprise that included a faint hope that I might somehow, she didn't know how, it would take a miracle, pupate and lift off from the wretchedness of our circumstances and take to the air. The expression irritated me and so did my mother's view. I pictured a scarecrow to myself as on the cover of the *Bachelor* or the *World of Style* with a red and white lined cape, a top hat on pomaded hair and a face one would probably call sheepish, though no sheep ever looked like that, a snob who went to the theater for social reasons, and that thought was so repugnant to me that it was enough to make me want to blow up every theater in the world. Later on, I learned that all this time my mother was writing letters in which she complained that I was spending this fine winter going to the theater in the evening. Was it a fine winter? It was cold and I was hungry. In the theater I was able to claim a free ticket, it was a claim I had managed to establish, and it had turned into a sort of right of custom that I defended over and over again even if I was surprised that anyone accepted it. I walked into the theater through the sandstone-pillared entryway that hinted at the classical origins of all culture, and perhaps also of the birth of tragedy. The pillars had received holes and scrapes from bullets exchanged by the Kapp volunteers and striking workers. This damage was like an open wound. Defenders and opponents of the republic had fallen here, but the majority of the theatergoers were inclined to view only the deaths of those young people who wanted the end of the republic and its hated flag as tragic and heroic. The others were forgotten like an unpleasant, embarrassing circumstance, and their friends and families were not theatergoers, except for Lenz, who was on the side of those who had won and lost. In his *Wan-*

dervogel garb, Lenz looked down from the upper circle, from Olympus at his opponents, but they no longer felt the need to look up to him: they reckoned him among the dead. The fake marble box office gave the theater the appearance of a public baths. Each time I went, I was both excited and dejected. The prospect of the play lent me wings, but the premonition of certain disappointment dejected me. The theater air was probably warming, but it didn't promise more than itself, a bourgeois spectacle. I made for the box office, fear in my heart, arrogance in my expression, I saw Fräulein Mannhart standing behind the cashier and supervising the allocation of free tickets, rigidly and implacably, and I felt certain that she didn't like me. From time to time my glance got stuck on her, not with hostility, I didn't have anything against Fräulein Mannhart and I certainly didn't want to upset her, but the thought that she was capable of damaging me made me look at her with curiosity, because the curiosity about her life, which in reality I did not feel, led out from me to her, and I scanned her puddingy matronly face for the truth about the gossip that was current about her in the theater, and I asked myself what would have possessed Emanuel to have slept with Fräulein Mannhart, and now put up with jealous scenes from her in his office. It never occurred to me that Fräulein Mannhart was suffering. Her much talked-about affair bored me, but when I stood at the box office, asking for my free ticket, and therefore in a position of some dependence on Fräulein Mannhart, then I thought her demand that Emanuel be faithful to her was ridiculous, yes, even the notion that he could have noticed her struck me as so improbable that I thought I read madness in the murky shimmer of her eyes, and I thought she had probably started the rumor herself. Fräulein Mannhart threw me my ticket, reluctantly, as if offended by my existence. I passed through the double-doors into the foyer, the still empty auditorium lay behind the open doors like a chiaroscuro cavern, offering refuge. I didn't flee into it though. I didn't avail myself of the chiaroscuro. I was not innocent. I was aware of my long, never-cut hair, my ripped, dirty, only suit, its patched elbows, the fraying, ankle-length trousers, my holey down-at-heel shoes, and I stood in the most prominent place in the passage, where my wretched appearance was multiplied by three mirrors, like a monument impossible to ignore. My position allowed me to take in the theater public to annoy them and to despise them. Along came the businessmen and shopkeepers, our creditors, who liked to send the popular actors hampers, because that had become the practice in our town, so that, when the baskets were handed over on stage, they could feel like patrons of the arts, after a heavy supper in their Sunday best, and their womenfolk vied in the public eye with the wives of professors in their jewelry and their dresses, a fight that was never won, because the members of the academic elite under attack were swathed in dove-gray plainness, disguising their penury as classic style. I eyed them sternly, hoping all the while to catch sight of Fräulein von Lossin. My challenge, which cost me palpitations to persist in, was leveled at Fräulein von Lossin. As she wasn't there yet, and might not come at all, I mocked the two theater critics of the town, the secondary school head of German who was employed by the Nationalist paper, and the elementary school teacher who penned reviews for the Social Democratic rag. Both turned up with their harpies of spouses, who terrorized them, but in the theater a strange bedazzlement came over them and they linked arms with them, both striding along like well-loved statues suddenly able to walk, and who over their too-tight tailcoats wore faces creased into plaster-of-Paris thoughtfulness. They were both prize boobies and had the same taste, they both lay adoringly at the feet of our leading lady Fräulein Danata, they were jealous of each other, and had hell to pay at home, but since they believed they were obliged to polemicize against one another, following the example of Berlin, after every premiere they produced weird fabrications, because as they didn't speak to one another and couldn't know what the other would write, their limited intellect led them, to their subsequent embarrassment, to write the same review, which did not represent what they thought, and which they had sweated up merely in a crazed effort to be more original than the hated rival. It was only in their praise of the adored woman that they were splendidly unanimous and so spurred one another on to exuberant paeans of praise, which led the theater community

to fear—with only a few dissenters, who instead preferred to
hope for the same outcome—that a star like Miss Danata would
be plucked from their midst and be shunted off to Berlin. And
there she was, she had turned up, there was magnificent theater in
the grimly provincial foyer, a blonde luminescence, Fräulein von
Lossin, I thought I recognized her, her strutting walk, her nose in
the air, I followed her at a little distance to the cloakroom, urgent-
ly and with heart beating fit to burst, I stood in the light, Lohen-
grin unrecognized and in disguise, as arrogant as she was, and
then I saw that the person who had attracted me and frightened
me had black hair, alien black hair, gypsy black, so black that the
black shimmered into blue, it was Baudelaire's goddess who was
there surrendering her coat, the phantom of the hemisphere in a
head of hair, not her, the damsel of the Ostro-Bothnian Gulf, it
was unbelievable, she must have dyed it, dipped her comb, her
brush in a pot of color and painted her bright tresses subfusc, but
it was her, Fräulein von Lossin, not Baudelaire's black magici-
enne, and it was me who was changing her, discoloring her dark,
setting her down in the jungle, in the equatorial backlands of the
poet, not because I found her any more exciting in such get-up,
no, her blond hair bound me more securely than Indian hemp,
but perhaps my illusion was an expression of the desire that she
be different, or it was an effort to break her arrogance, her stupid
estate owner's pride, because black, gypsyish, equatorially dark as
she was she was homeless and undressed, a creature of fantasy,
booty fallen prey to me, I was free to go up to her, throw my arms
around her, break her resistance right there on the cloakroom table, with all those ninnies watching, but no, nothing more needed be said and done, I was mute and stiff, and the dark lady was
mute and didn't move, and all words were dead, and silence alone
brought us together, united us in front of the theater, we melted
as the bell sounded for the beginning of the performance, the corridor emptied, and she went and didn't see me seeing her, and
there was her cousin, blue ribbon on his chest, pale-blue cap in
hand held high and straight in front of him, the Corps Pomerania, the hacked at scarred mouth, a George Grosz face, Fräulein
von Lossin took his arm and was blond and elfin in a lovely and a

repulsive way, an air- or water-sprite from Nordic mythology, already irradiated by a future as Frau Landrat or Frau Regierungs-president and a member of the board of the Deutschnationaler Frauenverein or the Luisenbund, and I thought I want to run away from this town, away from this country, flee, flee, and I traipsed in with everyone and found my seat.

I was all alone in my town. I was young, but I wasn't aware of being young. It meant nothing to me. It had no cachet. No one asked me for it. Time had stopped. It was mainly suffering. But there was no one like me.

I mooched around. I went places. I hung around on corners and squares. I caught the eye wherever I went. I meant nothing. I stood in the middle of the marketplace. I was useless; I liked that. I enjoyed standing in the marketplace. Just standing there. I had nothing to sell. Not even myself. I wasn't in the market for anything. I didn't want to take part. I despised them. I didn't know the going rates. I didn't ask about the price.

I affected a stoop. I wished I could have had a hunchback. I wanted to be an outcast. It was to be something visible. They saw it. I heard them and didn't hear them. They called out after me. They mocked me, why don't you get the doctor to prescribe you a haircut. I didn't have a doctor; I was proud of not having a doctor. It didn't concern me. They shouted, yah, who's a girl then! My shoulder-length hair stood for a better world. I took off my shoes, knotted the laces together, hung them over my shoulder, and went around barefoot.

And so I felt the town. It was under my feet. It was hard and cold. The others didn't notice. Many of them loved boots. They liked to march. They had lost the war. They gagged on their defeat and they hated the republic. They said, we ought to have conscription. They shouted, straighten out a few people. They held their hands in front of their eyes. They wished they could cut me in pieces. They all of them shared one face.

I wasn't sad. I had a good time. I was the knight of the sorrowful countenance. That was a gas. I longed for joys. I wanted brightness. I thought they were funny, eyes tight shut, creasing up their foreheads, invoking the iron time of the war, and forgetting the dead. I refused to laugh at them. I thought of the charnel houses that were our victories.

My style was gloom. I put up the fake-fur collar on my coat. That coat was my kaftan. I had spent ages looking for it. I put on a Russian tunic, and wore it buttoned up to the throat. I jammed the broad-brimmed otherworldly hat of a country priest down on my head. If I bothered with a hat.

A child in a dark stairway; it seized my hand, whispered Your Reverence. I was Raskolnikov. I was a character from *The Devils*. The one out of the basement. I had stood under the gibbet. The messenger had come in time. Reprieved. The empty noose still dangled.

I torched the town. Erdmann's department store burned. A bonfire in the night. The town hall burned. My family tree burned. That was good. The law courts were ablaze. I unlocked the prison. I distributed the goods from the shops to the poor and the prisoners. Everyone was given a book from Buggenhagen's bookshop. The money from the banks lay around on the streets. Little children played with the notes, made paper boats and floated them in the gutter.

Perhaps I loved the town. I turned it upside down. I wrecked its order. I pissed on its celebrations.

A Russian addressed me in Russian. I was thrilled. I was a disciple of Kropotkin's. The Russian was troubled. He was an emigrant. He was homesick for a different Russia. In summer I went around under an umbrella. The umbrella was as white as the baking sky. The umbrella had lily-of-the-valley-green panels. I was abroad in the tropics. The umbrella had a silver handle shaped like a bird. When a storm blew, the bird flew away in the wind. I was deathly pale; I had put rice flour on my face.

I would rest where I was in the way. I lay down on the street, in people's doorways. I sat on the steps leading up to monuments for the dead. I stretched out on grass verges put there to beautify the scene for the bourgeoisie.

Libraries attracted me. I haunted them, greedy and addicted. I was in love with the people who worked in them. I was irresistible, the librarians were helpless. They did my bidding. They opened their shelves to me, they parted from their treasures. I surrounded myself with script. I guzzled type. I forgot myself. I sat in the public square like a drunkard. The alphabet swept me away.

I was a caution to the city. I was an irritation. (I wanted to be an irritation.) The authorities kept their eye on me. The bourgeois periscoped me in the swiveling mirrors at their windows. They saw a sea monster. The authorities felt provoked, and requested a law to deal with me. Borstals blew their view-halloos for me. They had me in their sights. They surrounded me. They set traps for me, which I failed to fall for. I didn't do anything. I didn't hurt anyone. That was suspicious. That was wicked.

I wanted to be me, for myself alone. They pressed themselves on me. The town stripped itself bare for me. It was not decent. It had an underground. The police beat you. Judges were biased. The public official abused his office. The minister did not believe. The gym teacher was a sadist. The drinkers came along and unstoppered their bottles. Morphinists and cokeheads showed their wounds and offered me snow. Tarts bared themselves. Thieves invited me out. The anthroposophist climbed the steeple of St. Nikolai and screamed, You are the devil incarnate. When he throttled me, I saw the sea. It swung gray under a gray swinging sky.

Lenz was a Communist. The lost sheep was to be brought back to the flock. Lenz wanted to flee the flock. He was ragged. He ran around all winter in short trousers and bare knees. That bound me to him. We swam in the sea in November. Our bicycles stood propped against each other, shivering. On his bicycle was a red flag with the hammer and sickle. The peoples of the earth hearkened to the signal. The peoples hearkened to nothing. The sirens were silent. Back then, they were still silent. On my handlebars, as a token of respect to Lenz, I had tied a black rag, the proud black flag of anarchy. Lenz was murdered. It was the ones with the pinched faces who did it. There was a Huns' grave somewhere; there they bashed his brains out and buried him right away.

I was avid for drama. I travelled fourth class. I was a stickler

for decency. My head was full of books. The town slipped back-
wards on the rails. Into the fog, into the gray clouds, into the
snow, into lost time. The raised fist of St. Nikolai threatened one
more time. It was only later that I felt the scars. The compartment was for travelers with heavy loads. I sat on a basket. Sawdust
oozed out through the mesh. A hen clucked. A pig grunted in a
sack. The man who owned the pig asked me, what are you reading? I said Tairov, on theater as liberation. The man said, you'll
wreck your eyesight. It was snowing and cold. The train was un-
heated, the sky overcast. The man gave me a hard-boiled egg.

It was snowing. Berlin lay in snow. The Reich lay in snow.
The Stettiner Bahnhof was a cavern of wind and soot and a huge
commotion. It was Babylon; a place to leave. I liked the taste of
the air. I chewed freedom between my teeth. People were standing on streets everywhere, they were standing leaning against
walls, freezing and starving, they were unemployed, laid off, of
no fixed abode, they were the revolution. They stood around in
a different way to me. They didn't enjoy it. A column of them
formed up just of itself, there was no signal and no word of command, and I trotted along in the procession of those exhausted,
hopeless characters, and one asked me, have you got your card,
and I said, what card, and he shouted, your card of course, what
do you think, and I said, I'm not on the dole, and he pushed me
away and said, get away from here. The police arrived. The police
spilled out of their green cars. They fanned out. Whistles shrilled.
The police raised their batons. They scattered us. I took to my
heels with the others.

My heart quivered. It thumped proudly. This was it, I had
found it, this was what I wanted to put on, moral decency, theater as liberation, the street, the starving, the freezing, the desperate, the Red Flag, the song of the revolution. I quickened my step,
for a brief while I walked like someone with somewhere to go. I
thought of the play *Gas* by Georg Kaiser. I imagined the drama
Masses and Man by Ernst Toller in these grimy, sublime settings.
The Schlesischer Bahnhof was another cave of wind and soot and
din. It wasn't Babylon, though. It was a Hell for poor people with
nowhere to go.

At the end of the day I found myself in Grünberg. It was very cold. I made my way to the theater. I came in out of the snow. I saw lights. I heard singing. I felt warmth. The director was dressed in a houndstooth wool suit. He said, Ah, there you are. He said, Just as well. Someone was sick. He said, You can stand in. He said, Today in Salzach. He said, Tails. I looked at him, and then at my blanket roll that contained my comb, a spare shirt, and my books. It was all I had. He said, Oh, of course, your luggage hasn't arrived yet. He said, OK, go to the costume department. I said, "*Gas*". He said "Kaiser". He made a face. He said, My dear chap. He said, We'll see.

They were jolly. They were sad. They ate sandwiches. They were happy doing what they were doing. They weren't happy doing it. They toured, they sang, they hopped about. They slept together. They had little affairs. They were afraid to be alone at night. We froze on the bus to Salzach. They had worries. They weren't paid enough. They had children to look after. Their children were growing up. They weren't unfriendly. But they weren't my kind. I didn't open up to them. I crawled back inside myself.

They put me in my tails, which were much too long and much much too big, the big tails swamped me, they stuffed an iron-hard starched plastron under my waistcoat, they tied a collar and tie on me, my knees knocked together, they pushed me out on to the stage, there was a select society sipping water, the glasses sparkled, their mouths screeched, at night, when love awakens, the girls giggled, someone pointed me to the party I was supposed to arrest, he too was wearing tails, but his fit better than mine, I didn't know what his crime was supposed to be, I was playing a detective, what did I care, I put the handcuffs on him, I said in the name of the law, a sorry drumroll, the curtain fell, a rococo park, shepherds and shepherdesses gamboled on allegorical clouds to soothe the audience's feelings, and everyone congratulated me, you were very good, they said.

There was no one left in the house. Other houses had taken them in, comfortable houses, houses with stout locked doors, the houses of the bourgeoisie, houses full of warmth and sleep. All the lights were out. The snow lay there quietly. The moon had risen. The town was cozy and freezing. It was like a Christmas card. I got the picture. I was homeless. I had no money. I was making myself punishable by law. I dreaded the footfall of the policeman. The only sound was the frost creaking. I padded through the streets, looking for shelter. I found it. I climbed over a wall. I was in the cemetery. I found peace. I looked for a tomb for myself. I saw the crosses, the headstones, I read the legends on the graves. It was the old town that was asleep here. A respectable linen weaver. He was a kind host to me. I spread out my blanket; I laid my head on my books. I was at one with the world. I was satisfied. At intervals, to warm myself, I picked up my blanket, threw it over my shoulder, and ran alongside the cemetery wall, sometimes up a hill with a view of the sleeping town. I was visiting their ancestors; they in their beds had no idea. I shook with laughter, a wonderful hilarity. I imagined what if someone saw me wrapped in my blanket, how he would say he had seen a ghost in the night, did you know our cemetery is haunted. I loved being a ghost.

In the morning I was very cold. I washed under the icy torrent of a pump and drank the water. I was hungry. It was getting light. A friendly light was on in a baker's shop. The warm smell of freshly baked bread leaked out and the baker's wife stood behind the counter with bare arms. I didn't want to be bourgeois, but I was still in thrall to the prejudices of my upbringing. I felt so ashamed to be begging for a roll that I shivered in the oven warmth of the shop and said nothing. The baker's wife looked at me a long time, then she pointed at a poster next to her, and said, You must be with the theater. The rolls were fresh and crisp in a basket, and they were very near. I could have reached in and taken one. I said I'm a director. I said it in a haughty tone of voice. I said, *Gas.* By Kaiser, I said. My words, or the way I said them, seemed to alarm the plump, cheerful woman. It was as though it had taken her till now to see me for what I was, a boy, frozen, starving, with long hair, and all in black, like a priest. And if the baker's wife had only just in her kindness connected me with the theater poster behind her, which was for *Queen of the Night*, the operetta in which I had so successfully made my debut; now, warned by the words "Gas" and "Kaiser" she identified me with a quite different nocturnal character, presumably mad. She put out her bare arms to ward me off, and her mouth gaped wide to scream, while I, burning and blushing, with the sharp ring of the bell over the door still in my ear, ran away in terror.

In the theater the director in his woolen houndstooth was sitting on stage, rehearsing an old farce with his troupe. He looked at me. Have your clothes arrived? I looked back at him, or I wanted to look back at him, steady and demanding. But I felt queasy, and my head was spinning. He said, I don't have a part for you. He took in my coat, my fake-fur collar, which was disintegrating, my rumpled trousers, my unpolished shoes. I said, I've been taken on as a director. He contradicted me, but not raising his voice. You have not been taken on. I said *Gas* will be a success, the Berlin papers will write it up, Kerr and Ihering will come. He said, You're young. Youth didn't count. It enjoyed no respect. He said, My artistes … He pointed to the actors standing around on the stage dimly lit by a single bulb. I looked in the faces of petty officials trying to make a crust. He said, You see, they're all old enough to be your father, they won't take direction from you. He wasn't a monster. He paid my fare back.

With the money in my pocket, I went into the Black Eagle, or the White Eagle or the Red Eagle. I sat among those I'd previously slept among, honest linen weavers and merchants. I ordered belly of pork and local Polish wine. I was a young gentleman on the Grand Tour. I had come by coach. I was looking for adventure. The citizens of the place invited me back to their houses. They introduced me to their daughters. White sheets. I climbed in. Then India swam into my brain, and I decided I would go to sea.

The Oder was frozen over. The Oder barges wallowed in snow and silence. I travelled past Prussian fastnesses, Küstrin and Landsberg, bare exercise yards, sites of brutalization, hiding places of the Black Reichswehr, their Vehmic graves, planed down and forgotten. I saw it all growing back. I sensed it. Sitting in my compartment for travelers with heavy loads. It was an interval. They didn't have me. There was no running away.

Stettin smelled of herrings, but also of drowned bodies. The harbor was just outside the station. The roads to India were open. The drowned bodies wandered over the Lastadie, which was a harbor road. There were bars on it, warm and snug. You could get a grog against the howling wind. I didn't drink any grog. I didn't like the taste.

The youth hostel was in the attic of a school, a big red brick building, and the man in charge of the hostel had locked me up in the hostel and the school and had gone out, and I was all alone in the attic on one of a hundred beds, I had no light, only the moon shining through the dormer windows. Then I heard him. He came slowly up the stairs, not sneaking, calmly and proprietorially. I saw him in the dim light at the end of the dormitory, a man in a hunting hat, a green loden coat, and leather galoshes buckled over his shoes. I got up and ran to the other end of the room, to the staircase, I ran down the stairs and into the corridor downstairs that connected to the other staircase, and there he was again, on his side, with his hunting hat and loden coat and leather galoshes, on the third floor and the second floor and the ground floor, and I charged into a classroom, and I moved a bench up against the door, and I heard his footfall and heard him come to a stop, and then I couldn't hear him any more. I sat down at a desk, and I was a schoolboy facing the exam. I went up to the board, and I wrote down Liberty, Equality, Fraternity. That felt good. I felt calmer. I opened a window and jumped out into the schoolyard.

No ships were going to India. No ships were going anywhere. The sailors sat in the offices of the marine recruitment agency and waited for a berth. They waited and waited, and some of them had forgotten what they were waiting for. There were no ships going anywhere. The official behind the counter said, I'm sorry, it's no good. He said, Go home. I said, I have no home to go to. Then he wrote me down in his book and gave me a card. On the card, it said I was a cabin boy. I had a job. I was a member of the working class. I sat down among comrades. But the comrades said, get your hair cut, and they made the same joke about the doctor's prescription. They were bourgeois. They were bourgeois without houses and without property. They were bourgeois in everything but name and possessions. They were patient. They could take it. They disappointed me. I couldn't have stayed among them for long; they were suspicious of me; and I had nothing to eat and no shelter.

Then a man walked into the booking office who lived off the poor. He resembled a little the night hunter in the youth hostel. He was his brother. He was not terrifying; he was a scoundrel. He would pick a sailor, sit him down on a chair, lean down over him and say, sleep, sleep, and the sailor would close his eyes, his stout face would empty, and then the man said, raise your arm, the sailor raised his arm, the man said, you can't put your arm down, you can't get it down, and the sailor couldn't do it. Then the man said, you're a donkey, and the sailor scraped with his feet, and ee-awed like a donkey. The men laughed; only I didn't laugh. That was about all you could do with a sailor, and the hypnotist brought him round.

The man looked at me. Perhaps he looked at me because I hadn't laughed. I sat down on the chair, and he stared into my eyes, and in his face I saw hunger, fear and ruin, he was sick, his breath stank as he said to me sleep, sleep, sleep, and he made a terrific effort, sweat appeared on his brow, but he couldn't do it. Then I felt sorry for him, and I stood up on the chair and shouted, Lenin is speaking to you, arise, break your chains. The hypnotist raised his arms, wake up, he cried, wake up, come down, let's do something else. He looked at me questioningly. What do you think you're doing, he hissed in my ear. He massaged my temples, stroked me and said, be Jesus, arise and walk. With my best holy gait I walked to the sailors and they shrank back, and I blessed them. They were moved. I wanted to laugh, but then I was moved too. I wasn't hypnotized, I was just pretending, but something had happened to me, a spark had caught alight.

That evening and every evening we went down the Lastadie, we walked along the dock, past the ships at anchor, the ice on the water, far from India, we went from bar to bar, I would go in, I mingled with the drinkers, ordered something but didn't touch it, then he would come in, my master, call for attention, he would put someone to sleep, let him be a donkey, and then he would call me, by chance at the end he would call me, look into my eyes, breathe his putrid breath in my face, and stroke me. He told me to go and be Jesus and I was Jesus, and I walked among the drinkers and the whores and among the poor, and I blessed them and spoke to them and quoted to them from Scripture, and there was silence in the bar, you heard nothing but the sound of the money when my master passed the plate around.

I slept at her place. She took me back with her. She was a bargirl. I lay in her bed, in her little room, and she undressed, I saw her naked in the tarnished mirror, the glass told me that she was thin, a hungry little girl, and she saw that I was watching her, and she covered her breasts and her sex with her hand, and she turned away, and went to her cardboard suitcase and pulled out a shirt, a long peasant shirt of stout linen with long sleeves, she pulled it on, and it went down to her feet, she said, this is my shroud, she lay down beside me, and we slept and didn't touch, and it went on for a week or more.

Then the day came. The official behind the counter called out, cabin boy for the steamer *Eddy*, bound for Finland. I gave him my card, and he hired me. The doctor grabbed for my cock. He said, watch yourself with the women. He had dueling scars on his purple face. He winked at me. The steamer *Eddy* moved off. An icebreaker cleared our passage through the harbor ice. I saw the big open sea. An endless gravestone made of lead. I saw sea-battles, sinkings, bombardments. I saw the great shipwrecks ahead.

I wrote, my mother was afraid of snakes. She would see them on the brackish ground when we walked by the sea to the old estate. Grass ailed in briny puddles. The wheel of the salt-mill stood still. Rotten smells came out of the abattoir. I hated the town beyond the meadows, the famous outline painted by Caspar David Friedrich. I pictured it eaten by adders. But will anyone understand me? I mustn't admit that it doesn't matter to me whether no one understands or just one person, who of course would become terrifically important and mean that my endeavor hadn't been entirely in vain, even if I'm not sure myself whether I've captured something or even whether there was anything there to capture. But something happened, something is always happening, endlessly, there was once and there will be, that escapes our judgment, but this concerned me, no one else, even though when something is crushed I too am destroyed, or I observed something, it happened, I experienced it, I was a witness, it was an instant, a second, I could assume, would like to believe, there was a certain infinitesimal point in time, a specifiable event in the cosmos, already wiped away as though it had never been, were it not that it was stored in me, in the memory of some cell that might tire, sicken, dry out and die, but as long as I exist and am capable of thought, survive the terrible dangers, don't lose my mind, then there are records, data, as people say, that can be produced, accessed, on those frightening modern machines called electronic brains, and there is the recollection in an untidy tangle of a net, within reach, only woe if I lose the knack, the ability to operate the machine, if I mislay the key that summons up the past, sets it in indissoluble relation with the present and even the future, perhaps I could never handle the equipment nature endowed me with, and it's purely by chance that something stirs in me, takes a picture from the stock of preserved but forgotten, indifferent impressions, and endows it with significance, replays the long-past moment, creates it anew, or makes me feel it again. It's as if I were looking at an old photograph. I took it myself; or perhaps it's one of me. It's midday. A dingy day in January. My or their eyes tormented by the absence of sun. I was tormenting them or myself. Or what was I doing? Keep a face in a jar like fruit for winter, like meat for lean years, and finally, in the end, the metallic taste of iron rations and the strawberries of yore, the smell of the garden, the bed one summer morning still damp and fresh from the overnight thunderstorm, the tangle of little plants, the green overlapping leaves that formed the grayish vault where the tortoise liked to be, and the child, the giant, leans down, an omnipotent figure capable of expelling or of indulging, but the salted flesh had better not remember the calf, its gentle gaze, the warm dusty stubbly pelt, this is the hand that stroked you, my hand that took the knife that sliced open the throat, cut up the carcass, turns the roast, conducts the meat to my mouth, an ancient guilt sanctioned by nature, no longer unreflected, a process, as the history books gruesomely say. She is crossing the little bridge of rotten wood on her way to the Kastanienwall, it's her last walk, she's not to know that, the last time she's left her bed, a mild day like you sometimes get between hard frosts, the sky is purged of fog and snow and quivers with blue infinity, and that's what she's looking to me for, for help in dying, to provide her with meaning, her life now at an end is to have some meaning that she might understand or I am to justify her life, standing there on the bridge, in a coat ready for the trash, with my long-uncut hair, washed up, everyone said, without a future, just a word, a look, maybe a little reluctant gesture of my hand in the ripped gloves that she hopes for, and I say nothing, nothing at all, I look at her and I don't look at her, I don't move and I do move, though not towards her, more away from her, I know all that, I even laboriously suppress tears, but seeing her is annoying, it takes up my time, distracts me from something, from nothing, I don't know what and I think, this is important, and maybe then I started to talk, a lot of senseless stuff, I looked around as though cornered, up into the sky, silent like me, down from the bridge at the dirty ice in the Ryckgraben, launched into an exalted description of something that is nothing like whatever it is I am actually feeling. The hoop is placed around my chest, my eyes are burning and they grow wet, my hand is burning and it stops moving, it hurts so badly, because I felt nothing, it wasn't my death disrobing in the icehouse of shrubs under the bare chestnuts, I was already leaving her, or letting her leave me, Iphigenia as ever, even as I offered her my arm, led her home or pretended to, and thought instead of the trade I don't follow.

ONCE UPON A TIME
IN MASURIA

I live in Munich.
My desk is on the banks of the Isar.

Twilight, leafing through old papers. It's snowing. I think back
to my school days in Ortelsburg in Masuria, long ago now. There
was a war, then a difficult post-war period, then another war.
I lived in other cities.
There's a whole lifetime between me and Ortelsburg.

    ***

Lots of roads lead to Ortelsburg, or away from Ortelsburg. They
are tree-lined chaussees, dream-roads, forests and lakes from the
book of fairy-tales, now all for me.

    ***

I remember horse-drawn carts, and not many of them. From my
window I could see the road to the Korppeler Forest, to Passen-
heim, to Allenstein. That was the road that led out into the world.
In Allenstein, there were express trains to Königsberg, with wag-
ons-lit to Berlin.

    ***

I came to Ortelsburg with my uncle, with whom I lived as a
child. My uncle was an architect in the public service, and he was
moved to Ortelsburg. He was in charge of the Department of
Public Works, and he built churches, schools, town halls all over
Masuria, and dreamed of Palladio's miracles in Venice and Vicen-
za. That was how I came to be in Ortelsburg, and started school
there. My mother had no connection to the land or the people.

There was a silly saying she liked to quote: "Where culturia stoppeth, Masuria starteth."

***

Ortelsburg is now called Szczytno. Is the site of my childhood thereby lost, buried in wastes of time? I don't want to feel like a foreigner in a foreign place. I see Ortelsburg before me, I recognize and remember it, suddenly I am overwhelmed by the beauty of Masuria. As a child I took it all for granted. It's where I lived and played. Where I learned Latin.

***

And today? A bustling town. Cars, as everywhere else, car parks in place of hitching-posts, where the horses ate hay and oats. Pedestrian crossings, where I once went barefoot, as we all did. I don't like the tower of the town hall, which went up in 1936. The old town hall stood among trees outside the old Teutonic castle, a memorial honored the dead of 1870. The mayor knew every citizen by name. His policeman greeted you by touching the brim of his *Pickelhaube* helmet. It felt somehow cozy. But there was also a gendarme. He had a horse, and he worked for the Rural Council. Once, hidden in a rye field, I watched him. On a long rope behind his horse, he was leading some poor wretch into town. I was skiving off school, and kept my head down. Crows flew up over the wheat, the rye, the oat field, our daily bread.

***

Glimpsed behind roofs, from up on towers, the expanse of the Haussee. It feels as though it is only now that I can appreciate it, the miraculous friend of my youth. Bathing in the hot summers, the thick reed beds, the way you could row a boat into the forest. The boy felt protected in his isolation. Heavy thunderstorms. The reeds were said to keep thunder and lightning away. How the thunder rumbled.

***

On the opposite shore: the Catholic church, the castle brewery, the law-courts, the prison. What the Haussee could teach you.

***

My school was destroyed in the very first month of World War One, but was quickly rebuilt. A statue of Hindenburg, the victor of Tannenberg, stood beside the entrance. The school was renamed the Hindenburg Gymnasium.

How often I walked in through the gates past Hindenburg, and how often I shot out again. Was it that I had won something, or lost it?

They see a stranger, a foreigner, taking pictures of their school.

***

There were no buses in those days for pupils of the Hindenburg Gymnasium. My fellow-pupils who came in from the countryside, from the big landed estates, took the steam railway to class. Those of us who lived in Ortelsburg walked home.

***

Pavel, a Polish schoolboy, told me: "I live out in the country, so every day I have to travel twelve miles to school. No one likes going to school to study; everyone likes to go there to see his friends. I don't like homework, and maths and physics are my least favorite subjects."

***

Pavel's father is a self-employed builder. That's a prestigious thing in Poland. He has his own little house way outside town.

"There are four of us in the family: Mama, Papa, my sister Agnieszka and me. My mother is a book-keeper in a bank, and my father runs a small construction business. Agnieszka goes to school, same as me, and has a head full of marks and future jobs.

I don't know what I want to do yet. But I know I'll have to pass my exams. Exams aren't everything, though. I am being trained as an agricultural technician. If I fail my exams, I have a job waiting for me."

Pavel loves his little house and the town of Szczytno where he was born. But he would like to study in a big city somewhere, in Warsaw, or maybe abroad, in Paris or Berlin.

***

I am standing in front of a large, well-preserved building. It's our house. The house I lived in in Ortelsburg was called the official house. I didn't belong there. Our floor was divided between the flat where we lived, and the offices of the building department. Royal Prussian Department of Public Works. Of course I thought that was pretty impressive at the time.

***

In another wing of the big building, up in the attic, lived two ladies who taught at the girls' school, the Lyceum. They were artistic, and they played the piano—Mozart, Schubert, sometimes Viennese waltzes. For me that was something different, and I would go across and visit the ladies.

***

From the attic of the official house, I could look over the town and the countryside beyond. The lake was a placid gray. On the far side of it lay the poor people's part of town, Beutnerdorf, as it was called. Who might they be? Our washerwoman came over the ice in winter and did our washing.

Weeds and fences and tangled memories. My walk from the official house to the lake. How often I used to go! There was an enmity between the bathers and geese. As a boy I put on a shiny helmet, modeled on the one the Kaiser wore in photographs, to protect my eyes against pecks from the geese. We bathed naked in proud innocence, and we knew Ortelsburg mustn't ever hear about it.

***

From the attic, I saw the house of the master mason. This was a man wounded early on in the war, and invalided back in 1914. In his front garden he planted potatoes. At the back there was a path down to the lake. There was a rowing boat. And there sunning herself in an old rowboat, was Frieda! She was a girl who had been sent out into the countryside from starving Berlin. I was impressed by the fact that she came from Berlin, because that's where I wanted to go. That was in 1917. She didn't want to be called Miss.

At night we swam or rowed over the lake. It was August, and the night was thick with shooting stars; the sky was alive with them. Frieda from Berlin jumped into the cool water perfectly naked. She was taken from me. I dreamed of Frieda, the shooting stars, the cold water, and I wrote a story called "Frieda".

***

That was the line from Ortelsburg to Allenstein, from Allenstein to Ortelsburg. The boy looked out of the kitchen window of the official house and saw the trains go by. The summer of 1914 was beautiful and fine.

Already in June, military trains clattered through Ortelsburg on their way to the Russian frontier. The soldiers were not tricked out in bright colors. They travelled in field gray, and sang brave songs under gunfire. In the autumn, the carriages trundled back to Allenstein, with red crosses marked on their roofs, emblematic of blood. What do their grandchildren know? The days are still long, and the August nights full of stars.

The trains now follow a set timetable.

***

The view out of the old kitchen window of the official house. Is that still what it is? There are children playing in the yard. Time seems to have stopped—the same games, the same excitement, the same cries. The little detective follows the little criminal over the stable roof. Nothing seems to have changed for seventy years. Only it's the Polish version of the old games.

That old tree—I wonder if it remembers me? I planted a tree here somewhere, I wonder if that's the one.

I no longer remember.

***

The flight of stairs in front of the official house always struck the boy as terribly imposing. They were the mast of a sailing boat, an adventure playground, not without danger. Now they strike me as shabby and narrow. If people came with petitions to the office, the door of the flat was right there. Did I slide boldly down the balustrade on my way to school? Did I hurry off to school in the morning? I'd be surprised. It might be a fine summer's day or a walk in the dark in winter. Snowdrifts up to my chest. I walked alone. I had no friends on the street. Past the garden of the stern teacher, who grew flowers, fruit, and vegetables. His lessons kept the garden going. I passed the long railing of the Commercial Councillor's lathe factory. At six o'clock, a siren wailed, and the workers, a line of oppressed people, rushed in past the rails.

***

The way to school is a long way, then and now. Then I was met by Hindenburg standing at the gates of the stern building.

It still stands, with its cellars and corridors and stairs, and inter-connected classroom buildings, a child's fear of not being able to leave. Today the children greet a figure of some great Pole, he is their patron, their overlord, as Hindenburg was ours. Like any overlord, he's an intimidating figure. Hindenburg exhorted us to work and discipline, and above all obedience.

***

In the classroom, the slogan that—as in every classroom—means nothing.

Another classroom, older pupils, biology taught by a schoolma'am. Who are you, where do you come from, who is it, who brought you?

The girls and boys are a pretty picture, seen from behind. Alert, curious, eager, hungry for life and optimistic, on the creaky floor-boards.

***

On the noticeboard, some messages from the Union of Social-ist Youth.

The school would like to wish the pupils a happy holiday. Bye bye, school.

***

An historical picture on the walls. The fathers, the town fathers, the fathers of my generation, striding to the re-opening of the school following its destruction by the Russians in 1914. I can't remember if we took them seriously or not. They all wore top hats and dark undertaker's suits and strode smartly into the future.

***

27 January 1915, the Kaiser's birthday during the war. I was told to stand under the Kaiser's portrait in assembly and recite a poem. I stood there in a sailor's suit, and was the star of the morning:

***

The Kaiser is a gentleman
Who lives in Berlin town,
And if it weren't so far to go
I'd go there right away.

***

December 1918, the peace, no, the Armistice, was there at last, everyone had yearned for it to come, and no one wanted it. The survivors of the Ortelsburg Jagers came home from the field, and were to be welcomed back by the town. The soldiers looked dirty and dog-tired in their shabby uniforms.

The schools formed up into a guard of honor. From up on a rostrum a member of the Workers' and Soldiers' Council proclaimed a welcome. The Red Flag was flying. The survivors of the Front charged forward, raised their rifles, shots rang out.

The speaker from the Workers' and Soldiers' Council screamed: "Comrades!"

He wasn't hit, but a boy from elementary school who was standing next to him was shot dead.

***

The Ortelsburg cemetery was a favored walk for my mother. The cemetery was next to the Jagers' barracks, and the other side of it was the gasworks. Two lofty gasometers towered over the graves. It smelled of gas. The boy took the gas smell for the smell of death. It didn't frighten him. To him the smell of death was gentle and mild. It went with the soughing of the beautiful trees. The graves were carefully tended, the trees gave them shade.

Now the old cemetery is an abandoned field, gone to seed. Broken crosses and smashed gravestones still give the names of the dead, going back to the 18th century. Greetings to one of the dead, the apple of her eye is still alive.

***

One family grave: father, mother, and a couple of dead heroes. German military graves from 1914 and 1915, a couple of very young volunteers. They didn't have long to serve. Their parents died after them. They laid themselves down at the side of their sons. With pride.

***

A kitchen in the flat in the official house. How small it is. Kitchens have become so much bigger. Probably I am mistaken about that, in fact kitchens and kitchen ranges have grown smaller over time. This is where I built houses out of rope ladders and an ironing board.

***

Homework in the official house. The house broke up the lakeside idyll. To the boy, it seemed more like a prison.

Through the wall, the sound of piano music for four hands. The two woman teachers were there for life. The notes did not set them free.

***

His uncle is a Royal Prussian Structural Engineer. During the war he builds churches, it goes on for a long time. Building materials are in short supply. Many of the masons have died.

My uncle rides through the forest on an old bicycle. It is called an official journey.

***

Ortelsburg was small and rustic. On hot summer days, people went out into the forest. On ladder-wagons that were meant for gathering in the harvest, drawn by horses, they drove out into the Korpeller Forest. They sang patriotic songs of love and suffering, of long wanderings and heroic death. In the songs, the lives of gypsies were merry, the cavalry rode to their deaths, the sweet-natured forest animals waited for the huntsman's bullet, and under the bushes, in shallow trenches lay the young men of York von Wartenburg's Jagers. They were German songs, then they became Polish songs, every bit as sentimental. The singing was too loud for me. Nature was hushed before the storm. A paradisal wilderness. The business with Adam and Eve quite forgotten.

***

Picnicking in the forest was always peaceful and delightful. It might be a lavish affair, or something improvised. During the war, young people gathered kindling in the forest, even on school days. We lugged home sacks of it to Ortelsburg. I don't know what victory our harvest was supposed to celebrate.

***

The old water tower stands there all alone by the Haussee. At one time, it was at the very center of horse- and cattle-trading, and of all the pleasures of summer.

They put up the circus tent.

Outside the booths stood fire-eaters and the snake-charmer. There was a magician who sawed women in half, and turned rabbits into lovely girls. I worshipped the bareback rider, and, still more, her clever horse. The roller-coaster was a yelping path to the stars and to hell. All of that was alive once, and now it's not.

    ***

The Haussee was close to the water tower. Even in May, when the water was still cold, the lake made you feel like swimming. I leapt in, and went under. The water was cold, bracing and shocking. The shore was full of spots for loners and dreamers. That seems still to be the case. But, where the public baths used to be, there is now no swimming. The wooden piers and walks, the diving boards and changing cabins have splintered and moldered away. Now it's all nature again. It's better that way.

    ***

I was a solitary cyclist on the country roads round Ortelsburg, accepted by forest lake, and wild animal. Later, I had a friend I cycled with. We went into a bar in the forest, drank Masurian corn brandy, and in our magnificence showed off like grown men.

    ***

The young Poles cycle to bathe in the lake. It's a bright and sunny day and it's a merry gang of boys and girls that lives here now. Wild games in the water, screams and yells, no educator disturbs the pleasure they take in one another.

My teacher would have been appalled. Ten year-olds, we had stripped off, and ran around naked at the water's edge. Herr Dargel was most concerned. He was afraid of getting in trouble with the school governors.

***

Behind the station was the part of town that belonged to Commercial Councilor Anders, who owned almost everything. A couple of sawmills, where the forest trees came and were sawn to boards, two big steam mills that ground the corn from the fields to flour, to buckwheat kasha and to bread. In between, a couple of tennis courts and the Anders Park, which the great man had generously set aside for the public. The boy was in awe of him, he was like a king in a fairy tale, but close enough to touch. The villa quarter was like a town of its own. It was off the Willenberg Chaussee.

The Structural Engineer cycled around on his rusty wheels, and planted a church in a field, and a school on the edge of the forest.

***

The Anders Park was a rendezvous for young lovers. Beautiful, moral and a little desperate. The boys crept along behind the girls, and grabbed at their school berets. We called out "Please, Miss." Miss was fifteen years old.

***

Weeds sprout around the monument in the park. Perhaps it was the Kaiser on the cracked pillar or the great Bismarck. I had thought the firm upright figure on the pedestal was Commercial Councilor Anders. But, never mind. They are all gone into the world of light, the Kaiser, the steersman, and the Commercial Councilor.

But now Ortelsburg boasts a discotheque. It is situated on the old Kaiserstrasse, opposite the gymnasium. In the evening music starts to play, as loud as all the radios of Europe. The pupils of the Hindenburg Gymnasium and the new Lyceum trot across the road. They use "Du" with one another, and they dance together. Does that *son et lumière* take the place of the old Anders Park for today's lovers?

***

Daum's Brewery. The town of Ortelsburg and the surrounding countryside drank the well-regarded castle beer. In the castle lived a wild and lovely girl. She was supposed to be rich, and was chastely courted. I had no liking for beer. I stood outside on the road, and looked up at the high window. I was waiting for a girl-friend. The curtain in the window was drawn.

***

There was a bookshop in the town, "Zedler's Bookshop" it was called. I used to love it. I practically lived there. The pupils of the school went to the bookshop once a year. That was at Easter, once the promotion to the next class was assured, and you needed the books for the year ahead. I looked for different books, and took the schoolbooks home as well. I dropped them on my bed, and had them read by morning. Later, I read the other books.

I disturbed the bookseller because I asked about new publications that alarmed him. I gobbled up the Expressionist poets of the time. The bookseller ordered them for me. I said I would pay later. The bookseller waited for my uncle to come by, and presented him with the bill.

The Polish boy next to me is paying in cash. He is buying a history book. It was "Quo Vadis?" by Sienkiewicz. I could have hugged him.

***

The horse market in the town has remained important. There are still a lot of horses in Ortelsburg, and they still seem to me like old familiars. Once, the market was out by the lake and the water tower. Now it's just on the edge of town. People haggle as they used to do in the old days. The bid and the asking price are yelled out. A firm handshake seals the bargain. People trust each other. The horses watch patiently. I feel sorry for them, as I did in my youth. Will the new stable look after them, will the new fodder be to their taste, will the strange hand stroke them?

***

Next to the horse market is a new market for everything else. A market for poverty and indigence. The wares lie on quickly assembled tables; whatever a household can dispense with or a garden produce in the way of fresh fruit and vegetables. I think of the old days, and I ask, where is the fish? There is no fish in this market. It used to be that one would find them in a narrow alleyway leading down to the lake. Masses of them in tubs and barrels. They swam and shone, and I have to wonder: What's happened to them?

***

The old Jewish cemetery. Hardly anyone knows it's there, no one goes there. It seems abandoned, but not forgotten. The memory of the dead is cultivated. The paths are swept, the graves are not desecrated. The solitary traveller stands in front of the abandoned gravestones, feeling rather oppressed. The relatives were murdered or chased away. The wind of history blows over the grass. Peace maybe, resurrection hardly.

There used to be many Jews in Ortelsburg. They were devout or not devout. The devout Jews were from Poland, they had long beards and wore kaftans and black wide-brimmed hats. They looked like figures from a mystery play.

One non-devout Jew owned a business on the marketplace, and another one owned the first private car in Ortelsburg. It was very much admired. There were three Jews in my class; they only attracted notice on Jewish holidays, because then their places would remain empty.

***

The road to the abattoir was our schoolyard at the time our school was still in ruins.

A man would come out of the synagogue once a week, and cross the schoolyard to slaughter. We thought the man had a long knife under his kaftan. He looked interesting and a little chilling, a character in some horror play.

***

There was no anti-Semitism in Ortelsburg. I had a school friend I used to visit in the market pub that belonged to his father. The pub no longer exists, or the country people who drank there, or the father, or my friend.

There are no more Jews after the war. The war destroyed all the Jews, and now there isn't a single one left.

***

As a boy, I used to like going to church. If I was lucky, I would be all alone in the nave, and the organ would be playing. The space seemed holy to me. Sunday mass did nothing for me. It was a meeting of well-dressed property-owners. But on some days and at certain hours, a teacher from a different school used to preach in Masurian. I didn't understand a word of his sermon, and so I believed him. All the believers came, as they said, from the lower echelons of society. The women—the ones who crossed the ice in winter—wore headscarves. I liked them. I thought they are all our washerwomen.

***

The church has remained intact, inside and out. Intact the inscription concerning a German nobleman who left his money to the church for the greater glory of God and the Kaiser.

Not destroyed or vandalized either is a table for the dead of the 1914-1918 war. For Kaiser and Reich, loyally following the flag. There are many names, and all of them were young.

***

Pavel, the young Pole, says there are wars, and wars are stupid.

A situation whereby Poland, or in this instance Masuria could become German again is hardly imaginable to me. Although I can imagine anything, even that Germany might one day belong to Poland.

But not that, that, I think is impossible. I can't imagine a war either—no, I don't think there could ever be a war again.

***

In the spring of 1914, my mother went with me to see the Russian border. We reached the fortified German line in a beautiful and quiet forest landscape. The German soldiers allowed us to go on.

A few yards further were Russian soldiers. They were very bulky men in white uniforms, with wide, white flat caps. But the Russians would not let us over the border. They demanded to see papers, papers, papers. We had no papers. The Russian officer laughed. Well, why don't you go, but don't expect us to let you out.

The officer looked at my mother and asked: "Are you a spy?" We thought of Siberia. We knew the word, sometimes it appeared in the newspaper or in some famous book or other. We had heard of it. We turned back.

***

It was almost like a walk in the woods. We were in the middle of a forest. A curious wild animal emerged from the bushes. Not afraid. Birds in the branches. The little railway stations in the middle of nowhere.

***

There was an old joke in Masuria. The train stopped in Achotten. There was a traveler, from Berlin or Königsberg, getting impatient. He shouted out along the empty platform: "Enough Achotten!" In a temper, the stationmaster walks up and scolds him: "Enough Achotten is not enough Achotten, when you say enough Achotten. There is enough Achotten only when I call out enough Achotten." And the little man fills his lungs and yells out: "Enough Achotten!" And then the train goes on its way, from Achotten station, to Achotten town.

***

The station outside Ortelsburg. It was only at catastrophic times like declarations of war that I knew it to be so busy. In August 1914 we were in a refugee train, fleeing the "Russian steamroller." That was how it was always referred to in the press. We didn't know where the train was going, and no one knew whether the Russians would shell it, which had been known to happen.

***

At the end of his reign, the Kaiser once came through Ortelsburg. It was a short visit, an anonymous visit. Nothing official, the status of a rumor or a report.

I stood in the station looking at the Imperial train. It looked very modest. It was evening. Dusk falling. There was a light on in one compartment of the train. A curtain was drawn across. I thought, the Kaiser is having his supper now, and he doesn't want to be disturbed.

End

MICHAL AJVAZ, *The Golden Age.*
The Other City.

PIERRE ALBERT-BIROT, *Grabinoulor.*

YUZ ALESHKOVSKY, *Kangaroo.*

FELIPE ALFAU, *Chromos. Locos.*

IVAN ÂNGELO, *The Celebration.*
The Tower of Glass.

ANTÓNIO LOBO ANTUNES, *Knowledge of Hell.*
The Splendor of Portugal.

ALAIN ARIAS-MISSON, *Theater of Incest.*

JOHN ASHBERY & JAMES SCHUYLER,
A Nest of Ninnies.

ROBERT ASHLEY, *Perfect Lives.*

GABRIELA AVIGUR-ROTEM, *Heatwave and Crazy Birds.*

DJUNA BARNES, *Ladies Almanack.*
Ryder.

JOHN BARTH, *Letters. Sabbatical.*

DONALD BARTHELME, *The King.*
Paradise.

SVETISLAV BASARA, *Chinese Letter.*

MIQUEL BAUÇÀ, *The Siege in the Room.*

RENÉ BELLETTO, *Dying.*

MAREK BIENCZYK, *Transparency.*

ANDREI BITOV, *Pushkin House.*

ANDREJ BLATNIK, *You Do Understand.*

LOUIS PAUL BOON, *Chapel Road.*
My Little War.
Summer in Termuren.

ROGER BOYLAN, *Killoyle.*

IGNÁCIO DE LOYOLA BRANDÃO, *Zero.*
Anonymous Celebrity.

BONNIE BREMSER, *Troia: Mexican Memoirs.*

CHRISTINE BROOKE-ROSE,
Amalgamemnon.

BRIGID BROPHY, *In Transit.*

GERALD L. BRUNS, *Modern Poetry and the Idea of Language.*

GABRIELLE BURTON, *Heartbreak Hotel.*

MICHEL BUTOR, *Degrees. Mobile.*

G. CABRERA INFANTE, *Infante's Inferno.*
Three Trapped Tigers.

ARNO CAMENISCH, *The Alp.*

JULIETA CAMPOS, *The Fear of Losing Eurydice.*

ANNE CARSON, *Eros the Bittersweet.*

ORLY CASTEL-BLOOM, *Dolly City.*

LOUIS-FERDINAND CÉLINE, *North.*
Rigadoon.
Castle to Castle.
Conversations with Professor Y.
London Bridge.
Normance.

MARIE CHAIX, *The Laurels of Lake Constance.*

HUGO CHARTERIS, *The Tide Is Right.*

ERIC CHEVILLARD, *Demolishing Nisard.*

MARC CHOLODENKO, *Mordechai Schamz.*

JOSHUA COHEN, *Witz.*

EMILY HOLMES COLEMAN, *The Shutter of Snow.*

ROBERT COOVER, *A Night at the Movies.*

STANLEY CRAWFORD, *Log of the S.S.*
The Mrs Unguentine.
Some Instructions to My Wife.

S.D. CHROSTOWSKA, *Permission.*

RENÉ CREVEL, *Putting My Foot in It.*

RALPH CUSACK, *Cadenza.*

NICHOLAS DELBANCO, *Sherbrookes.*
The Count of Concord.

NIGEL DENNIS, *Cards of Identity.*

PETER DIMOCK, *A Short Rhetoric for Leaving the Family.*

ARIEL DORFMAN, *Konfidenz.*

COLEMAN DOWELL, *Island People.*
Too Much Flesh and Jabez.

ARKADII DRAGOMOSHCHENKO,
Dust.

RIKKI DUCORNET, *Phosphor in Dreamland.*
The Complete Butcher's Tales.
The Jade Cabinet.
The Fountains of Neptune.

WILLIAM EASTLAKE, *The Bamboo Bed.*
   Castle Keep.
   Lyric of the Circle Heart.
JEAN ECHENOZ, *Chopin's Move.*
STANLEY ELKIN, *A Bad Man.*
   Criers and Kibitzers, Kibitzers and Criers.
   The Dick Gibson Show.
   The Franchiser.
   The Living End.
   Mrs. Ted Bliss.
FRANÇOIS EMMANUEL, *Invitation to a Voyage.*
SALVADOR ESPRIU, *Ariadne in the Grotesque Labyrinth.*
LESLIE A. FIEDLER, *Love and Death in the American Novel.*
JUAN FILLOY, *Op Oloop.*
ANDY FITCH, *Pop Poetics.*
GUSTAVE FLAUBERT, *Bouvard and Pécuchet.*
KASS FLEISHER, *Talking out of School.*
JON FOSSE, *Aliss at the Fire.*
   Melancholy.
FORD MADOX FORD, *The March of Literature.*
MAX FRISCH, *I'm Not Stiller.*
   Man in the Holocene.
CARLOS FUENTES, *Adam in Eden.*
   Christopher Unborn.
   Distant Relations.
   Terra Nostra.
   Where the Air Is Clear.
TAKEHIKO FUKUNAGA, *Flowers of Grass.*
WILLIAM GADDIS, JR., *The Recognitions.*
JANICE GALLOWAY, *Foreign Parts.*
   The Trick Is to Keep Breathing.
WILLIAM H. GASS, *Cartesian Sonata and Other Novellas.*
   The Tunnel. Willie Masters' Lonesome Wife.
GÉRARD GAVARRY, *Hoppla! 1 2 3.*
ETIENNE GILSON, *The Arts of the Beautiful.*
   Forms and Substances in the Arts.

C. S. GISCOMBE, *Giscome Road.*
   Here.
DOUGLAS GLOVER, *Bad News of the Heart.*
WITOLD GOMBROWICZ, *A Kind of Testament.*
PAULO EMÍLIO SALES GOMES, *P's Three Women.*
GEORGI GOSPODINOV, *Natural Novel.*
JUAN GOYTISOLO, *Count Julian.*
   Juan the Landless.
   Makbara.
   Marks of Identity.
HENRY GREEN, *Back.*
   Blindness.
   Concluding.
   Doting.
   Nothing.
JACK GREEN, *Fire the Bastards!*
JIŘÍ GRUŠA, *The Questionnaire.*
MELA HARTWIG, *Am I a Redundant Human Being?*
JOHN HAWKES, *The Passion Artist.*
   Whistlejacket.
ELIZABETH HEIGHWAY, ED., *Contemporary Georgian Fiction.*
ALEKSANDAR HEMON, ED., *Best European Fiction.*
AIDAN HIGGINS, *Balcony of Europe.*
   Blind Man's Bluff.
   Bornholm Night-Ferry.
   Flotsam and Jetsam.
   Langrishe, Go Down.
   Scenes from a Receding Past.
KEIZO HINO, *Isle of Dreams.*
KAZUSHI HOSAKA, *Plainsong.*
ALDOUS HUXLEY, *Antic Hay.*
   Crome Yellow.
   Point Counter Point.
   Those Barren Leaves.
   Time Must Have a Stop.
NAOYUKI II, *The Shadow of a Blue Cat.*
GERT JONKE, *Awakening to the Great Sleep War.*
   The Distant Sound.

GERT JONKE (cont.), *Geometric Regional
Novel.*
Homage to Czerny.
The System of Vienna.
JACQUES JOUET, *Mountain R. Savage.*
Upstaged.
MIEKO KANAI, *The Word Book.*
YORAM KANIUK, *Life on Sandpaper.*
HUGH KENNER, *Flaubert.*
Joyce and Beckett: The Stoic Comedians.
Joyce's Voices.
DANILO KIŠ, *The Attic.*
Garden, Ashes.
The Lute and the Scars.
Psalm 44.
A Tomb for Boris Davidovich.
ANITA KONKKA, *A Fool's Paradise.*
GEORGE KONRÁD, *The City Builder.*
TADEUSZ KONWICKI, *A Minor
Apocalypse.*
The Polish Complex.
MENIS KOUMANDAREAS, *Koula.*
ELAINE KRAF, *The Princess of 72nd Street.*
JIM KRUSOE, *Iceland.*
AYSE KULIN, *Farewell: A Mansion in
Occupied Istanbul.*
EMILIO LASCANO TEGUI,
On Elegance While Sleeping.
ERIC LAURRENT, *Do Not Touch.*
VIOLETTE LEDUC, *La Bâtarde.*
EDOUARD LEVÉ, *Autoportrait.*
Suicide.
Works.
MARIO LEVI, *Istanbul Was a Fairy Tale.*
DEBORAH LEVY, *Billy and Girl.*
JOSÉ LEZAMA LIMA, *Paradiso.*
ROSA LIKSOM, *Dark Paradise.*
OSMAN LINS, *Avalovara.*
The Queen of the Prisons of Greece.
ALF MAC LOCHLAINN, *Out of Focus.*
The Corpus in the Library.
RON LOEWINSOHN, *Magnetic Field(s).*
MINA LOY, *Stories and Essays of Mina Loy.*
J.M. MACHADO DE ASSIS, *Stories.*

MELISSA MALOUF, *More Than You Know.*
D. KEITH MANO, *Take Five.*
MICHELINE AHARONIAN MARCOM,
The Mirror in the Well.
A Brief History of Yes.
BEN MARCUS,
The Age of Wire and String.
WALLACE MARKFIELD, *Teitlebaum's
Window.*
To an Early Grave.
DAVID MARKSON, *Reader's Block.*
Wittgenstein's Mistress.
CAROLE MASO, *AVA.*
LADISLAV MATEJKA &
KRYSTYNA POMORSKA, EDS.,
*Readings in Russian Poetics: Formalist
and Structuralist Views.*
HARRY MATHEWS, *Cigarettes.*
The Conversions.
*The Human Country: New and Collected
Stories.*
The Journalist.
My Life in CIA.
Singular Pleasures.
*The Sinking of the Odradek
Stadium.*
Tlooth.
JOSEPH MCELROY, *Night Soul and Other
Stories.*
DONAL MCLAUGHLIN, *beheading the
virgin mary.*
ABDELWAHAB MEDDEB, *Talismano.*
GERHARD MEIER, *Isle of the Dead.*
HERMAN MELVILLE,
The Confidence-Man.
AMANDA MICHALOPOULOU, *I'd Like.*
STEVEN MILLHAUSER,
The Barnum Museum.
In the Penny Arcade.
RALPH J. MILLS, JR., *Essays on Poetry.*
MOMUS, *The Book of Jokes.*
CHRISTINE MONTALBETTI,
The Origin of Man.
Western.
OLIVE MOORE, *Spleen.*

NICHOLAS MOSLEY, *Accident.*
Assassins.
Catastrophe Practice.
Experience and Religion.
A Garden of Trees.
Hopeful Monsters.
Imago Bird.
Impossible Object.
Inventing God.
Judith.
Look at the Dark.
Natalie Natalia.
Serpent.
Time at War.

WARREN MOTTE, *Fables of the Novel: French Fiction since 1990.*
Fiction Now: The French Novel in the 21st Century.
Oulipo: A Primer of Potential Literature.

GERALD MURNANE, *Barley Patch.*
Inland.

YVES NAVARRE, *Our Share of Time.*
Sweet Tooth.

DOROTHY NELSON, *In Night's City.*
Tar and Feathers.

ESHKOL NEVO, *Homesick.*

WILFRIDO D. NOLLEDO, *But for the Lovers.*

FLANN O'BRIEN, *At Swim-Two-Birds.*
The Best of Myles.
The Dalkey Archive.
The Hard Life.
The Poor Mouth.
The Third Policeman.

CLAUDE OLLIER, *The Mise-en-Scène.*
Wert and the Life Without End.

GIOVANNI ORELLI, *Walaschek's Dream.*

PATRIK OUŘEDNÍK, *Europeana.*
The Opportune Moment, 1855.

BORIS PAHOR, *Necropolis.*

FERNANDO DEL PASO, *News from the Empire.*
Palinuro of Mexico.

ROBERT PINGET, *The Inquisitory.*
Mahu or The Material.
Trio.

MANUEL PUIG, *Betrayed by Rita Hayworth.*
The Buenos Aires Affair.
Heartbreak Tango.

RAYMOND QUENEAU, *The Last Days.*
Odile.
Pierrot Mon Ami.
Saint Glinglin.

ANN QUIN, *Berg.*
Passages.
Three.
Tripticks.

ISHMAEL REED, *The Free-Lance Pallbearers.*
The Last Days of Louisiana Red.
Ishmael Reed: The Plays.
Juice!
Reckless Eyeballing.
The Terrible Threes.
The Terrible Twos.
Yellow Back Radio Broke-Down.

JASIA REICHARDT, *15 Journeys Warsaw to London.*

NOËLLE REVAZ, *With the Animals.*

JOÃO UBALDO RIBEIRO, *House of the Fortunate Buddhas.*

JEAN RICARDOU, *Place Names.*

RAINER MARIA RILKE, *The Notebooks of Malte Laurids Brigge.*

JULIÁN RÍOS, *The House of Ulysses.*
Larva: A Midsummer Night's Babel.
Poundemonium.
Procession of Shadows.

AUGUSTO ROA BASTOS, *I the Supreme.*

DANIËL ROBBERECHTS, *Arriving in Avignon.*

JEAN ROLIN, *The Explosion of the Radiator Hose.*

OLIVIER ROLIN, *Hotel Crystal.*

ALIX CLEO ROUBAUD, *Alix's Journal.*

JACQUES ROUBAUD, *The Form of a City Changes Faster, Alas, Than the Human Heart.*
The Great Fire of London.
Hortense in Exile.
Hortense is Abducted.

FOR A FULL LIST OF PUBLICATIONS, VISIT: www.dalkeyarchive.com

JACQUES ROUBAUD (cont.), *The Loop.*
Mathematics: The Plurality of Worlds of Lewis.
The Princess Hoppy.
Some Thing Black.

RAYMOND ROUSSEL,
Impressions of Africa.

VEDRANA RUDAN, *Night.*

STIG SÆTERBAKKEN, *Siamese.*
Self Control.
Through the Night.

LYDIE SALVAYRE, *The Company of Ghosts.*
The Lecture.
The Power of Flies.

LUIS RAFAEL SÁNCHEZ, *Macho Camacho's Beat.*

SEVERO SARDUY, *Cobra & Maitreya.*

NATHALIE SARRAUTE, *Do You Hear Them?*
Martereau.
The Planetarium.

ARNO SCHMIDT, *Collected Novellas.*
Collected Stories.
Nobodaddy's Children.
Two Novels.

ASAF SCHURR, *Motti.*

GAIL SCOTT, *My Paris.*

DAMION SEARLS,
What We Were Doing and Where We Were Going.

JUNE AKERS SEESE, *Is This What Other Women Feel Too?*
What Waiting Really Means.

BERNARD SHARE, *Inish. Transit.*

VIKTOR SHKLOVSKY, *Bowstring.*
Knight's Move.
A Sentimental Journey: Memoirs 1917–1922.
Energy of Delusion: A Book on Plot.
Literature and Cinematography.
Theory of Prose.
Third Factory.
Zoo, or Letters Not about Love.

PIERRE SINIAC, *The Collaborators.*

KJERSTI A. SKOMSVOLD, *The Faster I Walk, the Smaller I am.*

JOSEF ŠKVORECKÝ,
The Engineer of Human Souls.

GILBERT SORRENTINO, *Aberration of Starlight.*
Blue Pastoral.
Crystal Vision.
Imaginative Qualities of Actual Things.
Mulligan Stew.
Pack of Lies.
Red the Fiend.
The Sky Changes.
Something Said.
Splendide-Hôtel.
Steelwork.
Under the Shadow.

W. M. SPACKMAN, *The Complete Fiction.*

ANDRZEJ STASIUK, *Dukla.*
Fado.

GERTRUDE STEIN, *The Making of Americans.*
A Novel of Thank You.

GWEN LI SUI (ED.), *Telltale: 11 Stories.*

LARS SVENDSEN, *A Philosophy of Evil.*

PIOTR SZEWC, *Annihilation.*

GONÇALO M. TAVARES, *Jerusalem.*
Joseph Walser's Machine.
Learning to Pray in the Age of Technique.

LUCIAN DAN TEODOROVICI, *Our Circus Presents . . .*

NIKANOR TERATOLOGEN, *Assisted Living.*

STEFAN THEMERSON, *Hobson's Island.*
The Mystery of the Sardine.
Tom Harris.

TAEKO TOMIOKA, *Building Waves.*

JOHN TOOMEY, *Sleepwalker.*

JEAN-PHILIPPE TOUSSAINT,
The Bathroom.
Camera.
Monsieur.
Reticence.
Running Away.
Self-Portrait Abroad.
Television.
The Truth about Marie.

FOR A FULL LIST OF PUBLICATIONS, VISIT: www.dalkeyarchive.com

DUMITRU TSEPENEAG, *Hotel Europa.*
  The Necessary Marriage.
  Pigeon Post.
  Vain Art of the Fugue.
ESTHER TUSQUETS, *Stranded.*
DUBRAVKA UGRESIC,
  Lend Me Your Character.
  Thank You for Not Reading.
TOR ULVEN, *Replacement.*
MATI UNT, *Brecht at Night.*
  Diary of a Blood Donor.
  Things in the Night.
ÁLVARO URIBE & OLIVIA SEARS, EDS.,
  Best of Contemporary Mexican Fiction.
ELOY URROZ, *Friction.*
  The Obstacles.
BUKET UZUNER, *I am Istanbul.*
LUISA VALENZUELA, *Dark Desires and
  the Others.*
  He Who Searches.
PAUL VERHAEGHEN, *Omega Minor.*
AGLAJA VETERANYI, *Why the Child is
  Cooking in the Polenta.*
BORIS VIAN, *Heartsnatcher.*
LLORENÇ VILLALONGA, *The Dolls'
  Room.*
TOOMAS VINT, *An Unending Landscape.*
IGOR VISHNEVETSKY, *Leningrad.*
ORNELA VORPSI, *The Country Where No
  One Ever Dies.*
AUSTRYN WAINHOUSE, *Hedyphagetica.*
CURTIS WHITE, *America's Magic
  Mountain.*
  The Idea of Home.
  Memories of My Father Watching TV.
  Requiem.
DIANE WILLIAMS, *Excitability:
  Selected Stories.*
  Romancer Erector.
DOUGLAS WOOLF, *Wall to Wall.*
  Ya! & John-Juan.
JAY WRIGHT, *Polynomials and Pollen.*
  The Presentable Art of Reading Absence.
PHILIP WYLIE, *Generation of Vipers.*

MARGUERITE YOUNG, *Angel in
  the Forest.*
  Miss MacIntosh, My Darling.
REYOUNG, *Unbabbling.*
VLADO ŽABOT, *The Succubus.*
ZORAN ŽIVKOVIĆ , *Hidden Camera.*
LOUIS ZUKOFSKY, *Collected Fiction.*
VITOMIL ZUPAN, *Minuet for Guitar.*
SCOTT ZWIREN, *God Head.*